Firestorm

Firestorm

JAN NEUBERT SCHULTZ

CAROLRHODA BOOKS, INC. • MINNEAPOLIS

Carolrhoda Books, Inc.
A division of Lerner Publishing Group
241 First Avenue North
Minneapolis, MN 55401 U.S.A.

Website address: www.lernerbooks.com

Library of Congress Cataloging-in-Publication Data

Schultz, Jan Neubert
    Firestorm / Jan Neubert Schultz
       p.   cm.
    Includes bibliographical references.
    Summary: Maggie hates moving from beautiful Superior,
Wisconsin, to dusty Hinckley, Minnesota, in 1894, until she almost
loses her family to a forest fire that sweeps through the town.
    ISBN: 0-87614-276-5
    1. Fires—Minnesota—Hinckley—Juvenile Fiction. [1. Fires—
Minnesota—Hinckley—Fiction. 2. Hinckley (Minn.)—Fiction.
3. Moving, Household—Fiction.] I. Title.
PZ7.S3885 Fi 2002
{Fic}—dc21   2001000755

Manufactured in the United States of America
1 2 3 4 5 6 – SB – 07 06 05 04 03 02

Dedicated to the memory of the victims,
the heroism of the rescuers,
the indomitable spirit of the survivors,
and the charity of the compassionate
during the Great Fire of 1894

TABLE OF CONTENTS

THE TRANSFER
May 16, 1894

"No, Papa! Please don't make us go," pleaded Maggie, the catch in her voice almost choking her. She stared down at her dinner plate, its tea-leaf pattern blurring in the soft glow of the kerosene lantern as she tried to hold back tears.

Papa answered gently, "It's all settled, Maggie. The Eastern Railroad has transferred me. We have to move to Hinckley." He kept his voice low, private.

Gramma reached over to touch her hand, but Maggie snatched it away.

"We don't have to go," Maggie said. "We can stay here at the boardinghouse. Eddie and Jack, too." She looked at Papa through wet eyes. "You can always stay here on your Superior run." We can still be together then."

Papa rubbed his forehead with his large hand, and Maggie could see her words had hurt him. She was sorry. Almost. She took a quick deep breath and looked over at Eddie, who always took her side.

Her big brother's voice was sharp. "Don't be silly, Maggie," Eddie said. "I'll have to live in Hinckley too, now that I'm working for the St. Paul-Duluth Railroad. With Papa and me working for two different railroads, Hinckley is the only place we can all live together. We certainly can't keep two houses in two different towns." His mouth formed a tight line as he looked directly at her.

Maggie stared back. Eddie sat with his elbows on the table, his determined expression just like Papa's. They had the same blue eyes, the same direct gaze. Maggie turned away. He was only seventeen. He was not her father—he couldn't give her orders.

From the corner of her eye, she noticed Gramma, head down, unusually quiet, folding and refolding her handkerchief in her lap. Looking away from Gramma too, Maggie crossed her arms tightly across her chest.

She looked around the warm dining room, at the large maple table that had belonged to Mama's mama. With all its leaves, it had room for twelve people, more than enough space for Maggie's family and three boarders. An evening breeze crept through the open windows, stirring the ivory lace curtains and wafting away the remains of the cooking smells. The boarders had already left the table and had gone to their rooms.

Jack reached for the last chicken wing on the platter.

"Why don't you want to go, Maggie?" he chirped. "Moving to a new house will be great! No boarders, no chores." He bit into the wing and kept talking with his mouth full. "And Hinckley! Way out West in Minnesota. With Indians!"

"But all my friends are here," Maggie burst out, very close to tears. "I can't leave Suzy and Nancy! And what about school?" She would have said more, but stopped abruptly to keep from crying.

"There's a new brick schoolhouse in Hinckley," Papa said. "You'll make lots of new friends." A wide grin spread across his face and he stretched his arm out over the table. "And wait till you see the little home I've bought. Just right for us. You won't need to help keep a big boardinghouse."

Gramma tried again. "Home is wherever we are together, child." She looked over her round gold-rimmed spectacles at Maggie. "Our family will be together, and we will make new friends," she added, a little plea in her voice.

"You don't understand, and you don't care," shouted Maggie, glaring around at them. "I don't want different friends and a different house and a different school." Her hands tightly gripped the table edge, scrunching up the linen cloth. "I won't like it!" Shoving back the tall ladder-back chair, she ran from the room. "Mama wouldn't like it either," she shot back. Her hand grabbed the newel post, and she swiveled around it and raced up the stairs to her room. She heard Gramma gasp and Papa shush her.

Maggie ran into her bedroom and shut the door behind her, not quite a slam. She crawled up onto her bed and reached for her small needlework pillow. It was the last thing Mama had embroidered before she died, three years ago, when Maggie was only ten. A tear dropped onto the brilliant blue and lavender silk threads that traced bluebells and forget-me-nots. Usually she pushed memories of Mama away. Down deep. Remembering Mama still hurt too much. Maggie wiped the back of her hand across her eyes, brushing away unwanted tears. It must hurt the rest of the family too— no one talked much about missing Mama.

With a sigh, Maggie stretched her legs out across the wide expanse of her four-poster bed. Just a couple of days ago, she and Nancy and Suzy had sat here munching sugar cookies and laughing about school. Planning the new dresses they would have sewn. Planning to join the glee club. Nancy had tossed her brown curls and talked about which boys she would tease, sending Maggie and Suzy into fits of giggles at everything she had said.

Maggie burrowed down into the feather comforter, clasping the pillow tightly against her. Flickering gaslight from the streetlamps crept through the lace curtains of the window, casting dim dappled shadows across the white candlewicked spread. The breeze had freshened, bringing in the sound of lapping waves off Lake Superior and the tangy smell of pine trees and lake water.

By the open window, Mama's rocker squeaked ever so softly as the breeze gave it a gentle push. Maggie looked over at it, almost expecting to see Mama rocking there, her needlework in her lap. Unable to hold the memory back, she remembered—relived—climbing up on Mama's lap, Mama pulling her close, rocking her, singing to her. She could no longer hold the tears back.

How could her family want to leave Mama's house and all Mama's things? It would be like leaving Mama behind.

PROGRESS & PROSPERITY
Morning, May 27, 1894

Maggie stepped through the heavy oak doors of the Eastern Minnesota Railway Depot onto the covered platform. Instead of the familiar damp morning mist off Lake Superior, a smoky haze hung in the air. It seemed too hot for early morning.

The huge black locomotive looming before her hissed impatiently. Impertinent puffs of white steam escaped the engine and darted back past the coal car. The engine suddenly jerked forward, and a clank reverberated down the length of the track as another coach was joined to the commuter train. Startled, Maggie looked down the line. Redcaps dragged clattering carts—trunks and valises piled on helter-skelter—down the brick platform to the baggage cars.

The door of the nearest passenger coach swished open and Papa, tall and slim and wearing a dark blue conductor's uniform, bounded down the steps.

"Missy," he said, "it's moving day!" He hugged her

and swung her off her feet, right there on the platform. She squirmed out of his grasp and turned away from him, pretending to be interested in the switching, ignoring his use of his nickname for her.

Gramma bustled out of the depot, red-faced and breathing heavily in the hot dry air. Her black Sunday dress looked uncomfortable and her arms were laden with baskets, boxes, and bundles tied with string.

"Jules," she called. "Find a place for my breakables." Papa kissed her round cheek through the pile of packages, taking as many of them as he could handle.

"I trust you have the rest of my baggage safely aboard," Gramma said, peering over her little gold glasses, now slightly askew. "Here, dear," she said, handing several bundles wrapped in brown paper to Maggie. Unburdened, she led the way into the passenger car and stuffed everything below the seats Papa had reserved for them.

Settling herself in the seat facing Gramma, Maggie stared grimly at the goings-on outside her window.

"I have to tend to business," Papa said. "I'll have more time to talk when we're underway. Jack's seeing to the baggage." He spotted the engineer on the platform and hurried off to talk with him.

Gramma's taffeta dress rustled noisily as she settled herself into her seat.

"So, good," she said. "Tonight our family will be together in our new house. And I'll have a nice little kitchen and a cozy parlor . . . " Gramma chattered on aimlessly, her days of keeping a boardinghouse behind her.

Maggie gazed around the car's interior at the plump, red-upholstered seats, the polished wood paneling, and the brass lamps on the walls. As nice as the coach was, Hinckley was at the end of this trip, and there hadn't been any way she could change that. A wrinkle rippled across her brow and she tossed her head, her dark brown ringlets swinging back over her shoulder. She expected her new house wouldn't be as nice as this railroad coach. Probably it would be a lot smaller than their Superior house and wouldn't have brass lamps or carved woodwork moldings or an open staircase or a corner china cupboard. . . .

Passengers boarded, jostling about in the aisles with their baggage. The daily run from Superior, Wisconsin, to St. Paul, Minnesota, was about to get underway.

Gramma leaned forward, peering though the window.

"Where's Jack? Is he lollygagging again?" She grew flustered and fussy. "He probably thinks he'll ride in the caboose with your papa's cronies." She settled back with a huffy little snort.

Maggie wished she could ride in the caboose. Jack was only ten, and even though Gramma called him a sure and certain rascal, he got away with everything. Glancing back outside, Maggie saw Papa conduct the last of the passengers aboard, draw out his pocket watch to check the time, and give a final glance down the dusty depot platform. Calling, "All aboard," he leapt onto the metal step and leaned outward to signal the engineer.

Two sharp whistle blasts pierced the air, a long hiss of steam released from the engine, and a lurching jerk began the journey. Soon the train settled into a comfortable roll and sway. Maggie leaned back against the plush backrest. Black smoke waved past her window and a wayward spark winked by. By midafternoon, she'd be in Hinckley.

In no time at all, the train left the city behind and raced through thick forests. Tall stands of pine crowded the tracks, forming a beautifully lush green tunnel that towered over the railcars speeding beneath them. Maggie stared, entranced—she had never before seen trees like that. The forest was immense, so beautiful and wild. Nose pressed against the window, she watched the miles race past. In small clearings, along lakes and ponds, she glimpsed deer, black bears, and small furry animals. A moose standing in a swampy bay raised his head as the train steamed by, dripping wet water plants hanging from its mouth. Nonchalantly it watched an eagle swoop down to the water and soar off with a large fish struggling in its talons.

Maggie was disconcerted. This was all so lovely, not at all what she had expected. Was this what Hinckley would be like? Her imagination pictured a neat white frame house surrounded by towering pines, with deer grazing in a front yard that sloped down to a sparkling lakeshore.

"Eddie will meet us at the depot," said Papa, sitting down beside her and grinning across at Gramma. "Your new kitchen is all stocked, but we could eat at the Morrison Hotel tonight."

Gramma's eyebrows shot up. "Nonsense," she said, waving a lace-edged handkerchief. "Our first meal will be in our new home." She pursed her lips and looked over her eyeglasses. "Has the table arrived? Is it set up?"

Papa laughed as he stood up again. "It's all there," he said. "And I got some currants from the market, in case you're of a mind to have pie for supper."

"Of course we will," said Gramma, fidgeting.

Papa noticed Maggie staring out the window.

"Enjoy the scenery while you can, Missy," he said. "Hinckley's a lumber town, you know."

Maggie turned her head sharply. What did that mean?

"There's not much forest left," he explained. "The

land is nearly all cleared." He waved his arms again. "Hinckley's a busy, bustling town. New houses, hotels, stores, churches, a school . . . "

A businessman in a black suit and a string tie chimed in from across the aisle.

"The Future has arrived in Hinckley," his deep voice boomed. "Progress is on the move, and Prosperity follows." He puffed a long brown cigar, enveloping his head in smoky blue-gray haze.

Her heart beating wildly, Maggie stared back out the window. A prolonged whistle from the engine startled a deer watching the train passing, and it bounded back into the forest. Coal smoke billowed past the window, reflecting the glowing tip of the cigar. Maggie's glance caught her own reflection, framed with swirling black smoke and gleaming coals.

DUSTY, DIRTY, DRAB, & DRY
Afternoon, May 27, 1894

Maggie reached up to rub the tightened muscles at the back of her neck. Short shallow breaths escaped her as she stared out the train window. The magnificent forests were left far behind, and now manmade devastation was all her eyes could see, for as far as she could see. Where majestic white pine had once towered, jagged tree stumps and dry brush lay dead and dying. Lumber crews had claimed the virgin forest, industriously bent on harvesting the huge trees for their lumber companies. With a resounding whoosh, a one-hundred-foot tall pine tree crashed to its death, landing mere feet from the railroad tracks, setting the entire train to shuddering and shaking. Frightened, Maggie pressed herself back against her seat.

Like great fallen giants, white pines littered the forest floor. Like flies on a dead horse, logging crews crawled over them with axes and saws hacking branches and boughs off the still-quivering trees. Teams of draft horses hauled the stripped logs away, leaving the tree-tops and branches where they lay. Maggie's hands flattened against the window on either side of her face. How could the lumber companies be allowed to commit such destruction, such murder?

Farther down the line, temporary logging camps had sprung up, tents and wagons poking through scattered brush piles and stumps. Mile after mile, the train steamed through endless acres of slashed limbs and brush piles left behind as lumberjacks advanced into standing forest. Maggie turned to stare at her grandmother.

Gramma's red cheeks had gone white, her eyes widened almost beyond the lenses of her glasses.

"What is Jules bringing us into?" Gramma whispered.

The other passengers talked on as if nothing was wrong. Anyone looking out the window commented only on the prosperity forestry would bring.

Clang! Clang! Maggie jumped. The engine bell only rang for stops—were they already in Hinckley? She leaned close to the window, looking ahead down the tracks. A cluster of unpainted wooden buildings lay ahead. A lumberjacks' camp? A way station for supplies? Maggie dreaded even a short stop in this devastated landscape. Now she wanted to get past all this and on to Hinckley, to the white house in the forest she had imagined.

Papa stepped through the doorway at the front of the coach.

"Next stop, Hinckley," he announced. "Passengers bound for Hinckley will disembark in five minutes."

Maggie looked up at Papa, then back again out the window. The train slowed down. A tilted water tower and a shack—a depot?—appeared alongside the tracks. This was Hinckley?

"Gramma, Papa can't expect us to live here," Maggie said. "Tell him so!"

Gramma was still pale. She breathed deeply and exhaled slowly. "Let's wait and see what the house is like and the town. Your papa thinks it's very nice."

Stunned, Maggie stared at Gramma, who gathered up their packages and piled them in Maggie's arms. In a wordless daze, she followed Gramma off the train. A hot dusty breeze carried the scent of wood smoke and fresh-cut lumber. Maggie glanced up at a painted sign on the depot. *Hinckley*. Down the main street, unpainted wood buildings lined up crookedly, fronted by plank boardwalks. A dusty whirlwind whisked itself down the dirt road. Shouting, gesturing workmen scurried through the dust and wind from building to building, from wagon to buggy, yelling and waving and carrying boards and tools. Busy and bustling, all right.

A whistle tooted and steam hissed behind Maggie as

the train pulled out of the station, leaving her behind. Panic rose in her throat and she nearly ran after it.

"Gramma . . . ," she pleaded.

Papa hurried over, Jack bouncing along beside him.

"Here we are," Papa called. "It's only a few blocks to our house, but we've arranged a ride."

A farm buckboard wagon waited in the meager shade beside the depot, where Eddie supervised the loading of their baggage. Jack ran to help him, scrambling over everything. Papa hustled Maggie and Gramma up onto the wagon seat, talking nonstop about the newest buildings in town.

Maggie couldn't get a word past her tightened throat. Gramma leaned over to her and whispered, "Wait till we see the house."

Nothing changed as the tired old horse dragged the wagon through town, finally stopping in front of a small wood-frame house, this one with a porch vainly trying to give it an air of distinction. "We're home," said Papa, jumping off the wagon, lifting Maggie and Gramma down. Jack ran up the front walk, an uneven row of flat stones set in dry dirt.

* * * *

Maggie stared at the bare boards. Empty windows stared back. Papa's voice droned on, something about paint and shutters. Maggie stepped through the door and stopped short. The front room, though smaller than the parlor in their old house, contained all their things from Superior. But nothing was right.

Gramma's Turkish rug spread almost to the walls, too big for the room. The lovely walnut furniture lined up haphazardly around its edges, like discards at an auction. Maggie walked through to the kitchen. Mama's large maple table filled the far side of the room, even with most of its leaves removed. A shiny new black cookstove, its chrome handles gleaming, presided over the other half of the room. Making little clucking noises, Gramma opened cupboard doors and pulled drawers.

Papa pumped the hand pump on the wainscoted dry sink. Rusty water splashed and splattered as it hit the enamel basin. Proudly he pointed to the tin lantern suspended over the table, to the baking cupboard, to the back porch complete with washtubs and washboards. Jack already had his head in the oak icebox, checking out the food supply.

Maggie watched Gramma take a new white apron off a peg by the back door and bustle into the pantry. Maggie's hopes plummeted. She could see Gramma liked it, that she'd want to stay. Maggie turned her back on everyone. Noticing an enclosed kitchen stairway, she fled up to a short hallway that had four doors opening off it. The first door she opened revealed a small bedroom. Holding tight to the doorknob, Maggie looked at her own familiar bed, untidily made up by Papa. Her dresser, her commode, and her trunk stood silently. Lace curtains, lacking a curtain rod and sagging on a piece of string tacked to either side of the window frame, fluttered weakly in a breeze that smelled of fresh-cut lumber.

Mama's empty rocker stood on a faded rag rug in the corner.

Maggie's heart felt like a rock in her chest. Dimly she was aware Papa had tried to make it all look nice for her by stringing up her curtains and arranging her things. But his efforts hadn't helped. He didn't understand how much she loved and needed her home in Superior.

She stepped over to the window. Lifting aside the curtain, she looked out onto dust and dirt, dry streets, drab buildings.

There wasn't a tree in sight.

A WAY OUT
June 20, 1894

Maggie tossed the wet dishtowel over the clothesline and sat down on the back step. She untied her apron and used its clean hem to wipe the sweat off her forehead. Her gaze fixed on the backyard pump, but she didn't get up. She doubted she had the energy to pump water for a bath. It was so hot—had been ever since they had moved here. And there hadn't been a drop of rain either. Not even morning dew.

Leaning her head back against the porch post, Maggie stared down the alley at the neighbor's houses, all with backyards of bare dirt. She could hear Jack and Eddie roughhousing in the kitchen. No doubt Gramma was polishing the chrome on her stove. She'd soon have Jack out back, pumping water for her garden. Well water had kept alive a respectable plot of vegetables. The only garden in town, Maggie was sure.

The screen door squeaked as Papa came out and sat beside her. Maggie said nothing, staring at nothing.

"Gramma's garden is quite the wonder," Papa said. He pulled his pipe out of his pocket, then a leather tobacco pouch. "Most of the ladies in town are on her doorstep, wanting to buy or trade for her vegetables."

"S'pose so," Maggie said, wiping her neck with the apron hem.

Papa tamped the tobacco down into the bowl. "Guess by now she knows most everyone in town. She just told me to see if I can get some rhubarb at the farmer's market on my next Superior run." He struck a match on the sole of his boot and held it over the bowl, drawing on the pipe stem. A fragrant whiff of smoke curled into the air. "The ladies from the Swedish Lutheran Church are coming over next week," continued Papa. "She wants to impress them with her rhubarb pie." He chuckled softly.

Maggie didn't respond, but Papa went on in the same easy voice. "Jack's found a whole passel of rascals to run with," he said, "and Eddie and Tom Dunn are as close as brothers." He puffed on his pipe. "Have you met any girls your age?"

"No," said Maggie. "There's nothing to do here anyway."

"Tom Dunn told Eddie they just hired a girl about your age to help Grandma Dunn," said Papa. "Her name is Mary Anderson. She helps Grandma Dunn clean, do laundry, cook, and such." He leaned against the other porch post, puffing leisurely on his pipe.

Maggie was intrigued. Hired girl? Her age? If she could get a job like that, she could earn some money. She'd be good at it too, because of helping in the boardinghouse. And if she saved her money, she could go back to Superior and get a job there when she turned sixteen. Her heart beat faster and she sat up straighter. There were lots of rich folks with big houses in Superior who would hire her. She turned and looked at Papa.

"That sounds like something I could do. To keep myself busy." She kept her voice even and quiet.

Papa smiled. "I thought you might like to, at least until school starts," he said. "As a matter of fact, Dr. Stephan is looking for a housekeeper. He's a bachelor. His living quarters are behind his office downtown. You could stop at his office and inquire."

"Perhaps I will," said Maggie. She surely would. First thing tomorrow. Even if it took a couple of years, she would become the most efficient hired girl anyone could want. That would be her way out of Hinckley!

Papa stood and stretched, arms reaching almost to the porch roof. "I brought something back for you from Superior," he said, "from our old house." Stepping inside the door, he set down his pipe and brought out a burlap gunnysack. Opening it, he lifted out a handful of small branches, fresh and green and alive.

Maggie's hands reached straight for them. She touched, stroked, and petted the tender leaves. She put her face in the fragile branches, breathing in their green, growing fragrance. So sweet, so clean.

"The new owners let me dig these sprouts from around our old lilac bush," Papa said. "I told them you were a tad homesick and might like these growing under your window." His voice had a strange wistful tone.

Maggie carefully removed the tender shoots from the rough bag. "We must plant them tonight, before the roots dry out," she said. "Where's the shovel?"

As soon as Papa had a hole dug, Maggie knelt beside it, carefully spreading the fragile roots, filling in around them with handfuls of loose dirt. While Papa pumped a pail of water, Eddie came out and knelt beside Maggie. She tamped down the black soil.

"I remember when Mama planted these beside the old house," he said softly. "I held them just like this, while she tamped the dirt around."

Maggie sat back on her heels, staring at Eddie. He never talked like that about Mama. His eyes shone wet, but the edges of his mouth curled up. A tiny pain pricked in Maggie's chest—Eddie missed Mama too.

Papa knelt beside them, slowly tipping the pail to let the water trickle around the covered roots. "Mama loved growing things," he said. "Trees and grass and flowers. Just like you, Maggie."

Like me? Maggie had never made that connection before. She remembered Mama had been out in the backyard whenever she could, tending her flowers and lawn.

"Yes," she said slowly. "And she'd had other shrubs too. Bridal wreath, snowball, mock orange." The little prickle in her chest felt warm, good almost.

Papa chuckled a bit. "I remember many a time supper would be late, and Mama would come in from her flower garden, all muddy and laughing." Getting up, he and Eddie went back onto the porch and settled into the willow rocking chairs and talked about railroad schedules.

Maggie sat on the steps again, her back against the stair rail. The huge setting sun spread low red rays sifting through the hazy air. The fading daylight gave a softer tint to the houses and streets. She looked down at her brave little lilac stems, imagining Mama planting the original bush in Superior.

Then she shook her head and straightened her shoulders. One puny lilac branch that wouldn't bloom for years yet didn't make this town any better. First thing tomorrow she'd see if she could get a job as Dr. Stephan's hired girl!

NOTHING & NOWHERE
July 3, 1894

Maggie surveyed Dr. Stephan's kitchen with a critical eye. The dishes were all washed and neatly stacked in the corner cupboard, the polished wood floor gleamed, the rag rugs lay clean and flat. A beef stew simmered in a cast iron kettle on the wood-burning stove, ready for Dr. Stephan's supper. As Maggie hung her apron in the pantry, Dr. Stephan entered through the door leading from his office.

He sniffed the air, fragrant with roasting beef and potatoes. Though young for a doctor, he was handsome and dignified with his dark hair and mustache. Lifting the lid off the heavy black kettle, Dr. Stephan breathed in the moist warm steam and stuck a fork into the roast.

"Very nice," he said. "Someone certainly taught you housekeeping. Your grandmother, I assume."

Dr. Stephan had met with Papa and Gramma about hiring Maggie. Gramma had assured him that, even as young as she was, Maggie would do a good job. By the time he had finished a piece of rhubarb pie, Dr. Stephan was convinced, and Maggie had her first job as hired girl. She had also decided to add cooking and baking to her list of skills.

"Well then," said Dr. Stephan, replacing the pot lid, "tomorrow is the Glorious Fourth and you shall have the day off. I'm sure you'll want to go to all the festivities."

"Festivities?" Maggie asked. "What's planned for the Fourth?" Superior always had a big parade, a band concert, and fireworks over Lake Superior. What on earth could Hinckley offer?

"There's a parade, of course," said Dr. Stephan, his voice growing enthusiastic. "And a picnic in the Town Square. Baseball games in the schoolyard, and a dance at the Central Hotel. A splendid celebration."

Judging by his grin, Maggie guessed he'd attend everything. Gramma had said something about a picnic. Though, Lord knows, the dreadfully hot weather would make any celebration unbearable. As she left Dr. Stephan's, the parlor clock chimed the half-hour: 3:30. It was still early. Perhaps she'd go to the St. Paul-Duluth Railroad Depot. Eddie had been asking when she was going to come see where he worked. Just another drab shed beside a railroad track, she supposed.

Walking the few blocks east to the depot, dust and dirt blew into her face and billowed her skirts around her. She was dirty and disheveled when she reached the depot and too irritable to notice that the large, wood-frame building was neatly painted and the roadside graveled and raked. She slapped the dust off her skirts, thinking she'd need to beat her dress like a rug to get it clean again.

Stepping inside, the nice interior surprised her. A paneled lobby held rows of back-to-back chairs where passengers waited for the 4:00 Limited to St. Paul. A tall wainscoted counter partitioned the waiting room from the ticket office. Eddie stood behind the ticket window, wearing a white shirt, black bow tie, black suspenders, and black armbands around starched white shirtsleeves. He glanced up as Maggie shut the door behind her. His eyes looked green under his eyeshade and crinkled at the edges when he smiled at her. "So, little sister, you've finally come to see us."

A long, loud whistle pierced the air, announcing the arrival of the Limited. It pulled into the train yard, creating a hoopla of huffing, puffing, and bell clanging. Alongside the platform, the loading and unloading bustle began. People streamed in and out through the depot doors. Maggie stayed inside. Too hot to go back out again.

The engineer hurried into the lobby, heading for a side door.

"Hey there, Eddie," he called. "I've got fifteen minutes for a piece of pie and coffee." Maggie smelled coffee and glanced at the doorway the engineer had gone through. It had a sign over it that read, the Beanery. Was that a restaurant in the next room?

"Come over here," said Eddie, opening the half-gate of the counter. He ushered Maggie into the ticket office. "I'll show you around after the Limited pulls out."

He hurried to help the line of passengers waiting for tickets. Maggie went to the large bay window that gave a wide view of the platform and train yard. Tom Dunn was seated at the window, working at a long counter covered by schedules and charts. A telegraph machine clacked rapidly, and Tom wrote messages on a yellow notepad.

The engineer gave them a friendly wave as he hurried back toward his engine. Within fifteen minutes, the train had been tended, water reservoirs filled, coal replenished, and passengers and baggage loaded and unloaded. With an impatient whistle blast, the huge engine rattled southward down the tracks, all steam and smoke, bells and whistles.

This was the most excitement Maggie had seen since coming to Hinckley. But still, it was nothing like the vast, sprawling train yards and the large handsome depots in Duluth and Superior. She hoped Papa and

Eddie could advance to better positions. Someplace more important than this overgrown lumber camp.

When Tom's telegraph machine went silent, he leaned back in his chair and took off his eyeshade, brushing back his dark brown wavy hair. He winked up at Maggie, and she could see his eyes really were green. "Looking for a job?" he teased. "Want me to teach you telegraphy?"

"Always the flirt," said Eddie, coming over and good-naturedly punching Tom in the arm. "Let's straighten up for the next shift and then give Maggie the grand tour." Eddie smiled at his sister. "Want to see how well I run this station?"

"With a great deal of help from me," interrupted Tom. "Place would fall apart without my expert super-vision." He and Eddie grinned at each other. Each tak-ing Maggie by an arm, they swept her from the ticket office through the lobby to the restaurant and pointed up the stairway to the stationmaster's living quarters. "Think she'd like to see the baggage room?" Tom asked Eddie with a smirk. "Kind of crowded and dark in there, but she'd be safe with me. I'd protect her so nothing would tip and fall on her." Maggie giggled, wishing she knew how to flirt back.

"Who'd protect her from you?" laughed Eddie. "Let's get on home. It's getting close on to suppertime."

With sweeping bows, Eddie and Tom ushered her out the front door. They walked down the boardwalks three abreast, arriving first at Tom's house, where he lived with his grandmother. Eddie and Maggie went along in to say hello. A girl, slightly older than Maggie, met them at the door. Maggie realized she must be the hired girl Papa had told her about.

"Maggie, this is Mary Anderson. Mary, meet Maggie. Got any fresh cookies?" Tom said, all in one breath, heading past them to the kitchen. Eddie lingered a bit, smiling at Mary. Maggie was curious. Was Eddie wanting to talk with Mary?

Late afternoon sun came through the open door to lighten the dim foyer and cast spindly shadows up the open stairway. A mirrored coat tree against the wall reflected family portraits hanging opposite. Mary was very pretty, Maggie thought. Large blue eyes, long blond braids wrapped around her head. Maggie smiled, suddenly shy. She hadn't talked to anyone her age in weeks.

"Hello," was all she could think of to say.

"Pleased to meet you." Mary said, shaking hands all grown-up-like. "I've finished my work here and have to hurry home now to help my mother with supper. Are you going to the picnic tomorrow?" A dimple deepened in her cheek when she smiled.

"I think so," answered Maggie.

"We'll see you there," Eddie said quickly.

"Come in here and see me," called Grandma Dunn from the next room. "And let me meet the young lady." With a parting smile, Mary went out the front door. Maggie and Eddie walked into a large parlor, furnished with heavy black walnut furniture. Meager sunlight filtered through a big Boston fern that stood in a bay window hung with wine-red drapes. Tom came back through the kitchen door with a plate of cookies and followed them into the parlor.

"Tom, come set those cookies on the settee and light the lamps," Grandma Dunn called. She was short and plump, seated in a big rocker with her swollen feet up on a hassock.

"So tell me," she said to Maggie, "what's the fashion in Superior this summer? What's on the hats? Feathers? Flowers? Ribbons and lace? Can your Papa get some ribbon for me?" Big round cheeks spread wide with smiles and laughter. "When can you bring your Gramma to see me? Such a visit we could have!"

Maggie couldn't help but smile back, but Eddie cut the visit short.

"We'll bring Gramma this weekend," he said. "She'll probably bring along a pie."

"I'll have coffee ready," called Grandma Dunn as they left.

It seemed hotter than ever when Maggie and Eddie left the parlor and walked toward home. Passing the firehouse, Eddie noticed the doors had been left open. "Gone to another fire, I suppose," he said, peering inside.

"Nothing unusual," said Maggie, faking a cough. "There's more smoke in the air than dust lately."

Eddie shrugged. "Lots of brush fires all summer. But the volunteers keep them under control." He looked up at the hazy sky. "Sure would be nice to have some rain."

"Rain!" spluttered Maggie. "It never rains here. Instead of Hinckley, this town should be called Hades."

"Well now," said Eddie, "it's been awfully hot and dry this summer, but the weather will break one of these days. We'll probably get a downpour."

Maggie couldn't imagine Hinckley would ever have rain, but she didn't want to talk about the weather. Instead she said, "Eddie, how long do you have to work here before you can get transferred to Duluth or to St. Paul? Get a better job?"

Eddie stopped and stared at her. "What makes you think I'd want to leave? Hinckley's as important as anyplace. It's the railroads that are expanding this country, opening it up to new businesses and industry." He pointed toward the setting sun, shrouded in smoky haze. "If I went anywhere, it would be farther west, pushing back the wilderness."

Maggie took a step back, startled. "Eddie, how could you want to stay here? Hinckley is nothing and nowhere—it's ugly and desolate and awful. I'm going to leave as soon as I'm old enough."

They glared at each other a few minutes, standing only inches apart, but miles apart in attitude. Then they walked on again, not speaking. Maggie brushed an angry tear from her eye. "Dang smoke," she complained.

Back in Superior, she had loved the early evening. There, a light breeze off the lake freshened the air, the sinking sun set the waves a-glittering, seagulls circled the fishing boats returning to their docking, and the loons' haunting call beckoned the starry night. Mama had loved the loons. She could imitate their call. Tears welled up in Maggie's eyes, but she blinked them away. She straightened her back as she walked, determined that one day she'd return to her life in Superior.

The six o'clock whistle from the lumber mill shrieked. Maggie clapped her hands over her ears. Speaking in a voice straining to be companionable, Eddie said, "There's a boy who lives at the lumber mill. An orphan. He blows the whistles." Eddie pulled his railroad watch out of his pocket. "He's always right on time. Morning, noon, and night."

Maggie dropped her hands and stared at Eddie. An orphan living in a lumberyard! What kind of life was that?

THE GLORIOUS FOURTH
July 4, 1894

Maggie lugged the heavy laundry basket in through the back door. Though still early in the day, the clothes had dried quickly in the hot dry air. Too bad they always smelled of smoke. In Superior, they'd smelled of clean, fresh, piney air.

Gramma, her face red from the heat of the cookstove, opened the oven door and lifted out a blue enamel roaster with her mitted hands. A delicious smell drew Maggie. She set down the laundry and removed the roaster's lid, releasing a cloud of steam and a mouth-watering aroma of roasted meat.

"Fried chicken for the picnic?" she asked.

Gramma's cheeks got redder still. Without answering, she reached for a boiling saucepan and took it to the sink, carefully poured the hot water into the basin, then pumped cold water over the boiled eggs left in the pan.

Maggie looked into the roaster again. The drumsticks were very small.

"What is this?" she asked. She hoped it didn't have anything to do with Jack's forays into the woods.

"It's squirrels," said Gramma. She snatched the lid from Maggie's hands and slapped it back down on the roaster. "Don't tell anyone." She went back to the sink and cracked an eggshell against the basin's edge, then peeled the shell away from the boiled egg. "It's a sin what the meat market wants for a chicken," Gramma scolded. "Your Papa is going to have to build a chicken coop so a body can enjoy a chicken dinner come Sunday." She whacked another egg against the basin. "At least I can trade my vegetables for fresh eggs."

Maggie shook her head. Gramma and her trading. That vegetable garden was like money in the bank for her. There was so much garden, Maggie didn't know where a chicken coop would fit in the backyard. And if things weren't ugly enough, squawking, smelly chickens would do the trick.

"Back home," she reminded Gramma, "you could get whatever you wanted from the corner market."

"Hey, Gramma," called Jack, coming in the back door, "here's your milk." He set a small cream can on the big table. "Traded your green beans for this milk with the cook at the Morrison Hotel. Said he'd take any vegetables you could spare." He sniffed loudly and went to the stove, lifting the roaster lid. "Mighty fine chicken there, Gramma," he said, winking at her.

"Yes, you're right," Gramma smirked back. "Can't get that in the city." She glanced past him at a dark face pressed against the screen door. Jack had found a friend among the Chippewa who had a hunting camp at nearby Lake Mille Lacs.

"Wacouta, come in," she called, her eyes sparkling at another bartering prospect.

Slowly and carefully the Indian boy entered, wearing only leather leggings over his loincloth and a necklace of raccoon claws. His black hair was shiny, braided with colored feathers. Gramma stood behind her chopping block like a clerk behind a counter.

"So, Wacouta, did you come for some fresh vegetables? These young onions will put such flavor in your stews."

Expressionless but with black eyes shining, the young Chippewa held out a woven basket lined with soft leather. Gramma set it on the block and uncovered it. Maggie peered over her shoulder. Maple sugar! Jack was getting as good as Gramma at arranging trades.

Gramma emptied the sugar into a glass canister, filled the basket with onions, and handed it back to Wacouta. Turning to Jack, she said, "As soon as you draw water for the garden, you can meet your friends at the schoolyard ... "

The boys scrambled out the door before Gramma

finished speaking. The pump squeaked vigorously in the backyard, accompanied by the sound of splashing water hitting the galvanized pail. Gramma pushed the sugar canister to the back of the cupboard and watched the boys out her kitchen window.

"I declare," she said, "if we couldn't draw water from the ground, I think we'd perish." She sat down heavily on a kitchen chair and sliced boiled eggs in neat halves, scooping out the yellow yolks and mashing them with a fork. "It's always so hot. So dry."

"It was never like this in Superior," said Maggie, her tone sounding accusing even to herself. She added homemade salad dressing to the egg yolks, then salt and pepper and a touch of dry mustard as Gramma mixed it all together. Silently they stuffed the deviled yolks into the halved egg whites, laying them carefully into a flat, sectioned glass dish. Finished, Gramma sighed a deep sigh and began packing for the picnic.

"Droughts always come to an end," she said. "In six months we'll be knee-deep in snow. Just like Superior."

Maggie placed containers of food into the large wicker basket—the one they used to take to the rocky beach on Lake Superior. Certainly wouldn't need dry bread to feed any loons today.

Gramma took off her apron and reached for her sunbonnet.

"Let's go downtown," she said. "It's almost time for the parade." She unfolded the wicker handles and carried the basket out the door.

Maggie lifted the roaster, wrapped in dishtowels to keep the "chicken" warm. At the bottom of the porch steps, she set it down to check whether Jack had watered her lilac sprouts. He had. She wiped sooty dust from its few fragile leaves.

Firecrackers snapped and crackled down the street.

THE FESTIVITIES
July 4, 1894

"This can't be the park," said Maggie. The vacant lot had neither trees nor grass, but the dirt looked damp. It must have been sprinkled to hold down the dust. "Not even benches?"

Gramma pursed her lips and turned all the way around, searching for the perfect spot.

"We'll put our quilt on the ground behind the Town Hall," she decided. "The building should provide some shade in the afternoon." She strode across the lot and flipped her oldest quilt in the air, then let it settle down on the ground. She motioned to Maggie. "Put the picnic basket in the center to hold our spot."

Maggie set their belongings on the old quilt and looked around the deserted park. Other picnickers strolled around, choosing spots for their own quilts and baskets. Chattering like magpies, Maggie thought.

"Let's stand on the Town Hall veranda to watch the parade," she said. "We'll be out of the sun."

They followed the boardwalk and went up the few steps. Gramma elbowed their way through a talkative, excited crowd, edging her way close to the railing. Maggie, close behind her, soon realized the scant shade of the porch roof wouldn't help much. There was no breeze, and the smoke from the ever-present brush fires hung in the air.

"Maggie, got room for us over there?" Mary Anderson waved from across the street.

"Of course. Come on over." Maggie beckoned. Gramma looked questioningly over her spectacles at Maggie, who explained, "That's Mary Anderson, the girl who works for Grandma Dunn."

Mary, followed by her family, who seemed not to mind the crowded conditions, joined them on the Town Hall porch. Everyone introduced himself or herself, all talking at the same time. Gramma shook hand after hand, looking as delighted as she did with a good trade.

"Maggie! Hey!" Jack raced by with a group of boys, all of them waving.

Mary pushed up to the rail beside Maggie. "That's my cousin, Tony," she pointed out.

"Will Stanchfield is with them too," said Maggie. "They're at our house a lot. They know Gramma's cookie jar is always full of sugar cookies."

"Which they get after they weed and water my

garden," said Gramma. Her eyes twinkled. Evidently she thought cookies for chores was a good trade too. She wiggled in between Mary and Maggie to reclaim her place at the railing, but the boys were already a fair ways down the street.

"I expect they're off to see the new fire engine," Gramma said.

The sharp blast of the noon whistle from the lumber mill hushed the hubbub along the street, and everyone lined up to see who would lead the parade. Maggie was curious too. Superior had always begun with a community band, with shiny instruments and starched, pressed uniforms, playing a Sousa march.

Prancing down the center of the street, a beribboned black mare pulled an elegant four-wheeled buggy. An American flag bounced in the buggy-whip holder. Dr. Stephan drove, his associate Dr. Cowan riding beside him. Maggie waved to the driver, explaining to the Andersons, "My employer."

Dr. Stephan spotted her, smiled, and tipped his top hat.

"'Morning Alma, Maggie," he called. Gramma beamed back, waving her best lace handkerchief. A spanking new surrey followed the buggy.

"That's Mr. and Mrs. Brennan," said Mary. "Mr. Brennan owns the lumber mill. He's going to be the main speaker at the afternoon ceremonies." Another handsome surrey followed it. "And that's Angus Hay, the newspaper editor. He's going to speak too."

"Who's the pretty lady with him?" asked Maggie, watching a dark-haired young woman in the carriage smiling out from under a wide-brimmed hat.

"She's Angus's sister Clara," Mary said. "She teaches school at Lake Pokegama."

Mary watched them go by, wondering why Miss Hay didn't teach in a city.

"Such a lovely hat," remarked Gramma, looking pointedly at Maggie's and Mary's bare heads. A rowdy crowd of young men marched by next, waving and yelling. The crowd yelled back, some cheering and some jeering.

"That's our baseball team," Mary said. "The afternoon's games get pretty rambunctious, but you'll enjoy it."

Maggie raised one eyebrow. She'd prefer a band concert to watching this bunch of rowdies but was unsure about asking Mary if Hinckley had a band. Just then, another scruffy group sauntered down the street, playing squeaky fiddles and raspy mouth organs and wheezing concertinas.

Clattering and clanging their equipment, the Hinckley Volunteer Fire Department raced down the street, sporting spanking new uniforms with brass buttons. Eight men pulled a huge two-wheeled hose caisson and another ten men pulled the impressive new Waterous Fire Engine, all shined and polished for the parade. Yelling and hooting, the men stopped in the center of every block and roused the crowd into boisterous cheers.

Maggie, her shoulders jostled and shouts ringing in her ears, was a tad impressed herself. The engine looked like a huge round metal boiler on big wheels.

"How does the engine work?" she asked. "Where do they get water?"

A businessman standing behind Maggie said, "It's got its own hot water boiler and steam-driven pistons. The men roll out the hose, attach it to underground reservoirs, and the engine pumps all they need."

"The firemen train all the time," chimed in his companion. "In fact, they're about the best in the country. Entered the Firefighters Competition at the World Exposition in Chicago last year," he bragged. "Had to answer a fire call: get the engine up to steam, pull it ten city blocks, unroll and hook up hose, put out the fire. Did an outstanding job. Placed second in the country!"

"They could stop any fire!" agreed the businessman. "'Course, they get lots of practice fighting all the infernal little fires that flare up in the brush around here. Know their stuff, they do."

Maggie watched the volunteers pick up the wagon tongues and haul their equipment on down the street. There were more than twenty men. She studied the single engine and bit her lip, wondering if it merited all the confidence folks seemed to have in it.

The parade over, the crowds on the boardwalks spilled out onto the streets. Maggie and Gramma walked back to the park with the Andersons. Mary's family, now comprising several more relatives, including Mary's cousin Clara, settled beside them to enjoy their picnic lunches. Papa, off duty, joined them, and soon Eddie and Tom came by on a brief noon hour break. Ladies uncovered dishes and bowls and roasters and passed them around the crowd, everyone enthusiastically digging in.

"Hey, sister," said Eddie, "come along to the dance tonight. And Mary and Clara too." He winked at the girls and Tom waggled his eyebrows. Mary and Clara giggled, and Maggie felt her face blushing. She quickly poured lemonade from a crock jug while Gramma passed her potato salad.

Gramma got a little red too, when her roaster went around. Papa held up a tiny drumstick and gave Gramma a questioning glance.

"Young fryers," she commented. Maggie passed them quickly along without taking any. Jack and his buddies pounced down next to her, grabbing filled plates that Gramma offered.

"Maggie," said Jack between mouthfuls, "I'm playing in a ballgame later. Will's mother and Tony's mother and sister will be there. Can you come too?" He stuffed a whole deviled egg in his mouth.

"I'll see," answered Maggie, not too thrilled with the idea. If Jack were going to play ball all afternoon, she'd probably spend hours scrubbing dirt out of his knickers.

"Maggie," said Mary, "the new school is open today for the townsfolk to see. Let's run over and find our classroom for next fall." Her bright eyes twinkled from Maggie to Clara.

"Yes, let's!" said Clara. She jumped up and grabbed Maggie's hand. "Maybe we can claim our desks already."

Mary grasped Maggie's other hand, and they ran down the block to the new school, dodging picnickers and baskets. Maggie felt swept along again, not having given any thought to fall and school. Obviously, she'd have to go. At least she'd know some of her classmates.

A wide flight of steps led to double doors that opened into a wide hallway. The girls stopped and peered in. Quiet in there—no one about. Pigeons cooed up in the bell tower. They stepped inside. Maggie smelled varnish and, already, chalk dust. Four doors opened into the hallway, two on each side, those two separated by coat halls. Small desks lined up in a row in the first classroom they entered.

"This must be the first and second grade room," said Mary. "All the lower grades are on the first floor."

"Then let's go upstairs," said Clara. "Our classroom should be right above this one." She turned and ran out the door and up a stairway.

"Don't run in school," Mary yelled, running after her.

Maggie laughed, chasing after them. "Don't yell in school," she shouted.

At the top of the stairs, they grew quiet, cautiously entering their new room. Tall arched windows framed rather bleak views to the east and north. Polished wood desks with scrolled wrought-iron framework, linked by wooden floor slats, stood in neat rows like railroad cars on a track. Maggie touched the smooth finish on the new desks and looked around the room. Cupboards and bookshelves lined an inside wall. A large slate board spanned the front wall. Varnished hardwood floors, blue painted walls. Nice.

"The boys always want the back seats," said Mary. "We'll have to get here early the first day of school."

"So we can see their faces when they come in and see us all settled in the back row," said Clara. She slid into a wooden seat and grinned at Maggie, tapping the seat beside her. Maggie slipped into it as Mary slid into the next one.

"Maybe we can come in a day early," said Mary. "Offer to help the teacher." Maggie's smile widened. "Get our books into these desks."

Mary and Clara fell into fits of giggles. Fiddle squeaks and horn squeals screeched in through the open windows, and the girls ran to look out.

"The band's already warming up," said Clara.

Mary darted out the door and down the stairs. Maggie followed, hoping to hear a band concert. Folks had already ambled over to a raised platform decorated with red, white, and blue bunting, and the girls elbowed into position near the front. After a brief warm-up, the band played the national anthem, the crowd helpfully covering the band's mistakes with enthusiastic singing. It wasn't too bad, Maggie conceded. But that was all they played, disappointing her. They clanked off the stage, and Angus Hay stepped to the podium.

He welcomed everyone, grinning proudly out at the gathered crowd. First, he congratulated the townspeople on the rapid growth and prosperity of Hinckley.

"Our population is now over six hundred, plus another six hundred lumbermen," he enthused, thumbs hooked behind his suspenders. "Our new school is the envy of the county." He pointed an accusing finger down the street. "The only blight on our fair city is yonder gravel pit," he scolded. The railroads had dug a deep hole getting gravel for roadbeds, and it was now filled with about three feet of dirty scummy water. Angus slapped his hand on the bunting-covered podium, exclaiming, "The Eastern Minnesota Railway should do something about it!"

"Hear, Hear!" the happy audience responded.

"A few trees and grass would do more to improve this town than anything," Maggie complained to Mary and Clara. She had seen that grimy hole before, smack in the middle of town. Definitely disgraceful.

Mr. Brennan was next at the speaker's stand, and Maggie pushed forward through the crowd to see and hear better. What would Mr. Brennan say about all the trees he had cut down, the forest he had destroyed? Images of desecrated forest filled her mind.

The distinguished gentleman proudly recited statistics.

"Our lumberyard now extends over thirty-six acres. Over five hundred employees produce two hundred thousand board feet of lumber a day," he boasted. "There are twenty-eight million board feet of stacked lumber in our yards, awaiting shipment to all parts of America. Our fire-fighting equipment at the yard can stop anything. Every building has water barrels atop them, and there are mains and hydrants throughout the yards." Mr. Brennan shook his fist at the sky. "Fire would surely meet defeat at the Brennan Lumber Mill!"

The crowd roared and whooped and yelled.

Maggie stood silent, jaws clamped tight. No one cared what happened to the forest, they didn't replant any trees. Or worry about the wild animals and birds— how or whether they would live. No one tried to make this town livable. They didn't bother with grass or trees or flowers. Even the new school seemed like an obstacle now. It would take three years before she finished school and could go back home to Superior. How could she bear it till then?

Not saying good-bye to anyone, she pushed her way through the crowds, back to her house, up to her room, and shut the door. She climbed into Mama's rocker, clutching her pillow, not wiping away the tears that streamed down her face.

No One Seems
Too Worried
Morning, September 1, 1894

Not wanting to be late for work at Dr. Stephan's house, Maggie raced down the porch steps, stumbling on the flagstone walk. Irritated, wondering why it was still dark at eight o' clock in the morning, she glanced at the sullen orange ball hanging at the eastern horizon. It looked more like a full moon on a dark night than the morning sun struggling to rise above dark clouds.

Maggie stopped dead in her tracks, goose bumps tingling her arms. Those weren't dark clouds. It was smoke! She did a slow complete turn, scanning the sky. The entire sky was dark with smoke.

"Maggie! School starts Monday," said Jack, racing past her. "Take the day off."

"Wait, Jack!" Maggie called. "Look at the sky. There must be a big fire someplace."

"Not anywhere near here," Jack yelled back. "I'm going fishing with Tony and Will." He disappeared around a dark corner.

Maggie shouted after him, "Get right home if that fire gets close to town!"

She hurried on. Not much worth saving in this town anyway. Well, lives, of course. She gave a last glance at the sky before she went in Dr. Stephan's back door. It seemed to be getting brighter. The sun was red. Angry, though. It was going to be another scorcher.

Maggie bustled about the kitchen, washing last night's dishes, sweeping the floor. Gramma always said that keeping your hands busy kept your mind from fretting about things. Maggie kept both hands and thoughts on her chores till the kitchen clock chimed eleven.

Time to plan lunch, she thought. It was way too hot to start a fire in the cookstove. Maybe there was something in the icebox she could fix without cooking. Yes, there were cold fried potatoes and salt herring with vinegar and onions.

Another hour passed as Maggie tidied up the bedroom, pulling the sheets tight on the mattress, flipping the light featherbed back to fluffy. She carried the rag rugs to the back porch to shake the dirt out, then stopped to look at the sky again. Now the heavy air had an eerie yellowish glow. It was hard to breathe. She leaned out over the porch railing and looked up. That sky. It was getting darker again. Toward the south, the smoke clouds seemed to be swirling.

When it got this hot and thunderclouds swirled in the air like that, it usually meant tornadoes. But those weren't storm clouds. It was smoke. And it was definitely getting darker. Dr. Stephan came out onto the porch. "Strange sky, isn't it?" he said. "There's a big forest fire southwest of here. Fire Chief Craig called all the volunteers for a meeting."

"It won't get into town, will it?" asked Maggie.

Dr. Stephan looked worried. "No one thinks it can," he said. "People say a fire couldn't jump across the railroad tracks, what with their wide graveled shoulders. And tracks enclose the west, south, and east sides of town. And the Grindstone River is to the north." Dr. Stephan stared at the dark smoke clouds, piling one atop another. "No one seems too worried."

Dr. Stephan looked very worried.

"Run along home now, it's way past noon," he told Maggie. "If it gets any worse, you and your grandmother should go to the Eastern Minnesota Railway Depot. Take the afternoon train out of town."

Maggie raced home. It kept getting darker, like evening coming on. The hot air was very still, very calm. At least there was no wind to carry the fire. But then, how could the smoke clouds be swirling?

It was dark as night when Maggie burst into her front door. Darker yet in the house. Gramma was lighting the kerosene lamps. "Gramma, what's happening? What should we do?" Maggie cried.

Gramma looked up, the yellow glow from the lamp lighting her cheeks, darkening her eyes. Her eyes looked scared. The match she still held burned down to her fingers, and she quickly blew it out. Picking up the lamp, she walked out to the front yard, peering though the darkness, not seeing much beyond the lamp's light.

"No alarms have sounded," she said, her voice trembling. "Why is it so dark?"

Dark soft flakes began to fall from the sky. Maggie caught some in her hands. "Ashes," she said, showing Gramma. "There's a forest fire to the south. I think it's getting closer."

Shriek! The fire alarm whistle! "Let's go to the depot!" said Maggie. "Maybe there's an early train out of town."

"I'll get a few things," said Gramma, bustling back inside and upstairs. She went into her bedroom and set the lamp on her dresses, then reached to the top shelf of her wardrobe and brought down a small satchel. She put in the family Bible, a handful of pictures from her dresser, and a change of underwear. Maggie followed, trying to hurry her. Time they couldn't waste was being frittered away.

"Get your things," Gramma told her.

Maggie ran to her room and grabbed a few clothes and the bit of money she had saved. She looked wildly around the room, wondering what else to take. Mama's pillow! She snatched it all up and met Gramma in the kitchen. Gramma packed it all in her bag, stuffed a clean white apron on top, and snapped the clasp shut. Then she went around blowing out the kerosene lamps she had lighted.

"Forget the lamps!" yelled Maggie. A strong wind had blown up suddenly, rattling the windows. She hustled Gramma out the door, down the walk, down the street. Ashes were still falling, also dirty black soot and glowing cinders. The wind swirled it around them, picking up dust from the road.

"Hurry!" urged Maggie, grabbing Gramma's arm. "Look behind us!"

To the southwest, where the fire trucks had raced off to with their fire bells a-clanging, red flares and flames appeared against the black clouds.

"It's into town!" Gramma gasped. Neighbors ran out of their houses, calling to family members to stay together. Children screamed, parents yelled, dogs barked. Flames rose into the sky from distant buildings. The wind shoved them fiercely from behind, nearly strong enough to push them down. Gramma struggled to go faster in her long skirts, clutching her satchel. The depot was just a block away.

Whoot! Whoot! A train whistle!

"There's a train at the depot!" shouted Maggie, the wind snatching at her voice. A hot cinder fell on her sleeve and burned through the fabric. Maggie yelped and brushed it off, not stopping as she pulled Gramma through streets crowded with frantic screaming people who were running and shoving in all directions. The wind howled down on them, pelting them with burning embers that Maggie frantically brushed off herself and Gramma, stumbling as they ran.

Father Lawler raced past, going from house to house, pounding on doors. "Run for your lives! Save yourselves!" he shouted again and again.

He was one of the firefighters, Maggie realized, fright building up in her like steam in a teakettle. That meant the fires had gotten out of control—that nothing could stop it now. The whole town was going to burn!

Maggie kept running, nearly dragging Gramma. The hot air burned her eyes, her throat. The sky above them was dark as night, but flames from the distant burning buildings cast huge writhing red reflections off the black swirling smoke clouds. Flares and flashes and explosions erupted throughout the far end of town, creating fiery images that made Maggie think she was caught inside a burning coal stove, surrounded by flames encased in black steel.

"The depot's just ahead," she yelled back at Gramma. "Hurry! Faster!"

Maggie and Gramma burst through the depot doors and ran out to the back platform alongside the tracks. Maggie stopped short, almost jerking Gramma off her feet. Looming up in front of her, blacker than the sky, stood a huge locomotive, steam up and waiting on the siding. It faced south, its headlamp glowing through the darkened train yard. Relief flooded through Maggie. Gramma gulped in big lungfuls of air, bent over almost double.

Then Maggie looked south, the way the engine's headlamp pointed. But the intense light down there didn't come from the train. The entire southern end of the train yard was on fire. Boxcars at the far end of the yard burned fiercely. Even the wooden ties that held the rails in place were burning. Maggie nearly fell to her knees in panic

The train was facing south. The fire was coming from the south. The turntable at the southern junction was on fire.

The train couldn't turn around.

SIGNAL FOR DEPARTURE
September 1, 1894

"There's Papa! Wait in the depot, Gramma, out of the wind. I'll find out when the train will leave." Maggie jumped across the tracks, skirting yardmen who were hurriedly disconnecting loaded boxcars from the freight engine onto a siding. There were no passenger-coaches in sight.

Papa, the engineer, and the brakeman stood near the adjacent track, shouting at each other over the roar of the wind. Maggie stood beside Papa, listening.

"We can't go south, it's all ablaze," said the brakeman. "And the turntable's on fire, so we can't turn the engine around. Only way out of here is to steam backwards all the way to Superior!"

"But we can't leave until Best's passenger train arrives," insisted Papa. "He's coming down from Superior on the same track we came in on. If we leave now, we'll crash into each other." He struggled to pull out his pocket watch, coattails flapping in the wind. "Best's train is due here in fifteen minutes. All the telegraph lines are down so we can't contact him. We have to wait till he gets here, then we can both head back north."

"We'll need every car we can get," shouted the brakeman. He pointed to the far end of the train yard. "Over there's three empty boxcars and a caboose. The only ones not burning."

"Hook them to my engine," said Engineer Barry, "and start loading people aboard. When Best arrives, we'll connect our trains together." He looked down the street. "No time to waste."

Following his glance, Maggie's heart nearly stopped. People ran frantically toward the depot, dragging trunks, bundles of valuables, children. Horses and wagons careened through them, heading north. Everyone yelling and screaming. Fire had reached the far end of the street, flames swooping down onto the buildings.

Would there be time for the passenger train to get here? Time to board? Time to escape? The wind howled like a living creature, a banshee intent on devouring the town. Maggie put her hands over her ears. Her face felt hot, dry, burned. She rubbed her smarting eyes. Opening them, she stared down the tracks into smoky, swirling blackness.

A light!

A light stabbed through the dark.

"Papa, look there! The train's coming!" She grabbed Papa's arm and pointed. They couldn't even hear it. The furious winds and the roar of flames overpowered the noise of the engine.

"Thank God!" said Papa. He ran toward the advancing locomotive, swinging his lantern. Brakes screeching, the train pulled up alongside the depot, its frightened passengers staring wide-eyed out the coach windows. Engineers, brakemen, and conductors from both trains ran toward each other between the tracks, shouting over the wind, now a blistering hot gale. Papa waved Maggie back to the platform.

Too anxious to go inside, Maggie turned to watch, tightly gripping a platform post. In front of her, a fireman disconnected Best's engine and drove it to the water tower. Of course—he needed to fill the water tank in the tender car—water was needed to drive the steam engine. The fireman stood atop the rounded steel tank of the tender and wrenched the tower's waterspout down, struggling against smoke and wind. He dropped to his knees as a blast of superheated air swept through the train yards.

Maggie ducked behind a loaded baggage cart as the wind struck her, scared more for the fireman than for herself. He had to get water! The engine couldn't make steam without water. She wiped her sleeve across her face and peered through swirling smoke.

The fireman struggled to his feet, lost his footing, and fell partway off the tender. He scrabbled back atop it, crouched, pulled off his jacket and tied it over his head. Leaning into the wind, he grasped the spout and manhandled it into the tender opening. The water flowed, leaking and splashing as the wind twisted the spout, but in two minutes the tank was full. He jumped down and eased the engine back to the depot. Maggie followed to the edge of the platform, watching through watery, smoke-filled eyes.

Switchmen dashed between cars and coaches, coupling them together, creating a train consisting of three freight cars, a caboose, and the five passenger coaches that had formed Best's train. Engineer Barry's engine was in front, Engineer Best's at the end, both engines still facing south. There was no way to turn them northward. Barry, pulling in the lead, would be the engineer in charge. Best would engineer the back engine, pushing from behind and applying brakes when he needed.

The engines would run in reverse, back north along the track they had come down on. Two brakemen, holding lanterns, would sit on the forwardmost part of the first engine. They would watch for damaged rails and dangerous windfalls, because the engine's headlamps were useless pointing backward.

Not waiting for the clanking cars to be coupled, panicked people streamed aboard, climbing, pushing, shoving, and shouting. Maggie ran to get Gramma from the depot. Papa and the other conductors stood by the entrances to the coaches, keeping people from trampling each other, making sure women and children boarded first. He got Maggie and Gramma into a passenger coach.

Maggie grabbed his sleeve as she stepped onto the metal step. "You're coming too, aren't you, Papa?"

"Yes, Missy. I will," he answered. "I'm going to get all my passengers to safety."

Maggie and Gramma crowded past people scrambling for benches.

"Are you all right, Gramma?" asked Maggie, pulling Gramma down on a seat beside her. Gramma breathed in short fast gasps. Her face was a blotchy red. She didn't answer but nodded briefly.

Maggie turned to look out her window. People and animals stampeded the length of Main Street, fire licking up the buildings they ran past. Flames leaped higher, jumping from building to building, setting them instantly afire. Walls were devoured in an instant, and Maggie could see the furniture burning inside. She saw great whirling balls of fire fly through the air, igniting everything they crashed against. It wasn't dark anymore!

Whoot! Whoot! The first engine blew its whistle twice, the signal for departure. The train jerked forward, then jerked to a sudden stop. Engineer Best, in the rear engine, had stopped them with his air brakes! Why? The coach was jammed, not even room to stand in the aisles. Howls and cries rang through the car.

Maggie pressed her face against the hot glass of the window. That's why Best stopped! People were still climbing and scrambling to get aboard. Dr. Stephan stood right outside, handing crying hysterical children up to Papa.

Whoot! Whoot! Another jerk forward, another abrupt stop. The depot whooshed up in flames, the southern end of the train yards completely ablaze. People kept coming, arms reaching out. Some fell in the streets.

Whoot! Whoot! Barry's engine was too far up the tracks for him to see the people still scrambling aboard. Again and again. Jerk. Stop. Jerk. Stop. Maggie couldn't breathe, the intense heat seared her throat, and her eyes smarted and teared. They had waited too long. They wouldn't make it.

Slowly, agonizingly, the train inched ahead. Then a bit quicker, jerkily, pulling hard. Maggie held her apron over her mouth and gasped in hot air. She looked out the window. Were they really moving? She felt small jerks, small pulls forward.

Still people ran toward them through streets of fire. Staggering, their clothes afire, they fell to the ground and were swallowed up by the smoke and dust layering the road. Buildings exploded and collapsed around them. Flames hurled forward. The train inched ahead.

Galloping out of the inferno, a crazed horse raced toward the train, its rider reaching, stretching. Her face pressed against the window glass, Maggie saw arms reach out from the railcar's open door. The horse's head, eyes wide and bulging, nostrils flaring, sprayed Maggie's window with frothy sweat.

A fireball whammed into a building alongside the track, exploding it with a whoosh of flame and gases. With a scream, the horse bolted away from the train into the flames, carrying its rider along.

Maggie choked. She gulped for air, swallowed smoke, coughed, and gagged. She leaned backward and gathered a breath of air into her lungs. Outside her window, ferocious, furious flames whirled and swirled against the glass.

Piercing through all of it screamed the mill whistle. Wheeeeeet! Wheeeeeeet!

Long. Loud. Hopeless.

The orphan boy.

UNLEASHED & UNHARNESSED
September 1, 1894

Maggie doubled over in her seat, hands over her head to shut out the cries and screams that ricocheted through the overcrowded coach and through her head. How could they even hope to escape? The fire had engulfed the town in minutes, overtaking desperately running people and panicked horses. It would overtake the train too.

One sound pierced Maggie's fear—Gramma, moaning. Maggie raised her head. Gramma groaned softly, her body rocking back and fourth, her apron over her face. Maggie reached around her shoulder, pulling her close.

"The train's moving, Gramma. Can you feel it?" She struggled to keep a quaver out of her voice.

Bracing herself, Maggie braved a look out the window, back into the town. Huge flaring sheets of flame consumed what was left of Hinckley, licking and lapping at everything in its path, howling with fury at the trainload of people attempting to escape. The fire became a demon, a flaming red demon, flinging fire bolts ahead of itself, reaching long arms of fire toward the train that ran but a few city blocks beyond, pursuing it on winds of tornadic force. Maggie stared, helpless and hopeless, into its maw. Surely it would devour them.

The train rocked forward, a shuddering staggering gait. Gradually it steadied itself, picking up a bit of speed as it crossed the trestle over the Grindstone River. Maggie stared wide-eyed down at the river. People were still alive out there! Running into the river—throwing themselves into the shallow, sluggish water. Maggie moved forward to shield Gramma's view, should she look up.

Suddenly Maggie was thrown forward as a series of jerks rocked the train. She glanced wildly around the car—people were flung forward and back and would have fallen had they not been so tightly packed. The train was slowing! Maggie looked frantically back out the window—they had passed the river. The train shuddered to a stop. Why? Why would it stop? Had something happened to the engines?

Then Maggie saw them. Clamoring crowds of people running toward the train, waving their arms, screaming for the train to wait. All along the length of the train, arms reached out of coach doors and boxcars and pulled people aboard, lifted babies and children from outstretched arms. Other hands grasped the parents and pulled them in. People seated in the coaches struggled to open jammed windows too small to pull anyone through, then slammed them shut as smoke whooshed in. Gasping, crying, coughing, and choking, more people jammed into the coach, nearly thrown off their feet as the brakes released and the train bolted forward. Maggie turned around in her seat, pressing her face against the window to see what lay ahead.

Flames!

A stand of unharvested timber, whipped by gale-force winds, burned fiercely on both sides of the track. Fear pounded through Maggie's veins. She couldn't move or speak. Gramma sobbed beside her. Mustn't let Gramma see this. Maggie held her tightly, trying to steady Gramma's trembling. Gramma curled over tighter than ever, and Maggie hoped she would keep her face in her apron.

The train roared full steam into the forest fire. Walls of flames crackled and snapped and snarled at the train racing through its fierce heart. Like lightning, flashes of light flickered over and around the interior of the darkened coach. Shadows leaped and danced against the walls. Maggie gaped at the people staggering around her. They looked like their faces were on fire. Maggie gasped—even breathing hurt. The air seared everyone's lungs, parched their mouths and noses. But everyone could still scream. Ragged, jagged screams from parched throats.

"The wind is behind us!" shrieked a distraught voice. "It's in a straight line with the tracks! We have a corridor of escape—we can go right through!"

Maggie shook her head vigorously. Go straight through? What if the tracks curved? What if the wind changed direction? What if burning trees fell on the rails? Maggie thought she would start screaming.

But Gramma was shaking and her shoulders heaved. Maggie choked down her own screams and gripped Gramma tighter. Hungry flames beat against the windows, but the glass held. The train charged on and through them. Roars of engines battled roars of furious fire.

A loud screech and a wave of smoke and a clatter of steel wheels whooshed into the coach as the door opened at the far end of the car. From the enclosed vestibule that connected the coach behind them, Dr. Stephan entered, quickly shutting the door again. A little girl clung to his neck.

"Mrs. Peterson!" he yelled, eyes searching the chaotic crowd. "Mrs. Peterson! Here's Sarah!" He struggled through the packed center aisle.

Maggie sat forward, still supporting Gramma. A young woman, face and hair and clothing scorched, reached out both arms, crying too hard to talk. They came together right by Maggie's bench. The child clutched at the mother. "Mama! Mama!"

Thank God, the little girl had her mama again.

Mama. Maggie's vision got black around the edges, the noises seemed to fade away, and the flames receded. Her head felt light, her body numb.

Gramma's shrill voice pulled her back in an instant.

"Dr. Stephan!" said Gramma, leaning away from Maggie. "Where's Jack? Have you seen Jack? Is he aboard?"

Maggie's head jerked up. Jack! She stood up, still dizzy, and reached for Dr. Stephan's arm. He took her hand.

"Maggie. Alma. Listen," he said, voice deep and steady. "I haven't seen Jack yet, but families are separated and scattered all over the train. Did you see him get on board? Was he with you?"

With a wail, Gramma threw the apron over her face and cried. Long shuddering sobs.

"No," Maggie rasped. "I haven't seen him since early this morning. He was going fishing with his friends." Her knees trembled, and she felt too weak to stand much longer. Dr. Stephan frowned, his hand tightening on Maggie's.

"If he was near water, he may be safe."

Maggie sagged back onto the bench.

"Mary Anderson is in the caboose, her folks are in the baggage car," said Dr. Stephan. "Clara Anderson is in another passenger coach, but I haven't seen her parents or brothers yet. They might be in a boxcar. It's sooty as all get-out from the coal dust back there." He paused a minute. " Jack may be on the train too. Maybe you'll find him when we all get off at Superior."

"Superior?" asked Maggie. "Won't we stop before then?"

"Most likely not," said Dr. Stephan. "At least not for more than a few minutes to get coal and water. We need to get beyond the forests." He glanced around the crowded car. "All these people will need a place to stay, to get medical help. Superior and Duluth are our best refuge." He released Maggie's hand. "I have to tell the Gustafsons I saw their son board at the last minute."

Maggie sat back and scrunched her eyes tightly shut, overwhelmed with fear for Jack. Suddenly her heart lurched, remembering Eddie, hoping desperately that he had gotten out on his train, that the Limited had gotten there in time. Gotten away in time.

Gramma was quieter, crying softly. Maybe praying.

Again the door banged open at the end of the coach, admitting howling winds and hot smoky air and a clamorous racket of steel wheels on steel rails. Maggie opened her eyes. Papa! She gulped a smoky breath and shook Gramma.

"Papa's here!"

Gramma wiped her eyes on her apron and looked up, eyeglasses perched on her forehead. Everyone riveted his or her attention on Papa in his blue uniform.

"We're pulling ahead of the fire, folks," he shouted. "God willing, we'll make it to Superior tonight." Questions hurtled at him from all sides. Papa raised both hands, palms outward. "I don't know who all is aboard. You'll have to wait till we get to Superior. I don't know the condition of the track ahead or the path of the fire. But take heart. We are drawing ahead and away."

Gramma breathed easier and leaned her head against the bench rest. Maggie squirmed out of her seat and followed Papa out into the vestibule between coaches. There was a short loading platform at the ends of each coach where people boarded, and when joined together, flexible leather curtains on each side made a safe passageway between cars. Papa disconnected the leather sides and pushed them back so they could see out.

The intensity of the fire had lessened. The air cleared somewhat. Behind them, fires blazed in scattered areas, the wind whipping it through brush piles. Maggie shuddered. The demon fire could yet bear down on them. They were only safe for the moment.

"Where's Jack, Papa? Did you see him? What about Eddie?" Maggie stared back at the fires. Flares and flashes leaped from treetop to treetop, chasing the train.

Papa's voice was dry and scratchy. "Eddie may have gotten out on the Limited. Maybe Jack ran to his depot and got out with him, if he was on that end of town." He paused. "If the Limited got into Hinckley. It was due about the time we left. Maybe a bit later."

"But there wasn't any time after we left," Maggie cried. "Everything was on fire by then!"

"We ran through fire," Papa said. "The Limited could have done the same thing." His voice cracked. He put his arm around Maggie, and they stared out the doorway, not saying anything more.

They passed by telegraph poles all on fire, like candles burning their entire length. The wires snapped and twined around the poles like twisting snakes. The train slowed again, then picked up speed. Whistles signaled back and forth between the engines. Papa leaned out and looked ahead.

"There's a bridge ahead. Barry must have slowed to make sure it's safe to cross." He paused a minute. "Looks like it's burning."

A second later, they were on it. Flames reached up from its timbers and snatched at Maggie's dress hem. She shrieked and jumped back, pulling her skirts around her. Within another few seconds, the burning bridge was also behind them.

Gradually they drew ahead of the fires. It seemed brighter. Natural light, not firelight. Maggie leaned slightly outward and looked back. The sky was very dark behind them. Rolling, rumbling, swirling black smoke clouds, red flashes darting through them like heat lightning.

Just like it had been this morning in Hinckley.

Don't Look Down
September 1, 1894

Whoot! Whoot! the lead engine signaled. Papa grabbed his lantern and leaned out the doorway, waving it.

"Sandstone, just ahead." he called. As the train pulled into the station, Papa jumped off. Engineers, conductors, and brakemen leaped off all the cars and ran to the small wood-frame depot alongside the tracks, taking shelter from the wind under the covered platform. The Sandstone stationmaster came out of the depot followed by his telegrapher and ticket master, everyone shouting over the hot gusty wind. Maggie jumped down and ran up behind Papa.

"Hinckley's destroyed by fire!" yelled one of the conductors, pointing frantically backward. "Sandstone will go next. Connect any cars you have. Sound an alarm! Get all your people aboard!"

The stationmaster frowned, looked south at a dark sky lit here and there by red reflections.

"No worse than it's been all summer," he said. "It'll

burn itself out before it gets this far." His fellow work-ers agreed with him, nodding their heads.

Maggie stared at them, stunned. How could they not realize the danger? She turned toward the south. Sandstone, high on a bluff, afforded a grim view of the black clouds and red flashes back at Hinckley. She clutched her skirts as the strong hot wind snatched at them. How could these people ignore the signs? Couldn't they see?

Engineers Barry and Best had no time to argue.

"What's the condition of the trestle?" they both demanded.

Trestle? Maggie turned and looked up the tracks. Her heart lurched and she grabbed her throat. Ahead loomed a huge gaping canyon—the river gorge, spanned by a narrow one-track bridge. The wind howled hungrily around them, growing stronger and hotter as they talked, dropping sparks and cinders. Crackling and snapping, a small brush fire flared up in the woods opposite the tracks.

The engineers exchanged grim looks.

"To stay means certain death," said Barry. "The fire is right behind us. We have to take our chances on the trestle."

"As quickly as possible," agreed Best. Everyone scrambled back to their positions, Maggie on Papa's coattails. Barry's engine released two screaming whistle blasts, and steam hissed through smoke as they pulled away from the station.

An elderly signalman at the trestle windmilled his arm, waving them across.

"For God's sake, keep going!" he yelled. "It's eight hundred and fifty feet across, and the wooden support beams are already on fire, but you can still make it!"

Maggie and Papa, back on the coach platform, leaned outward to watch. Smoke gathered around them, a thick inky mass that swooped down with a deafening roar, whirling itself about the trestle, engulfing the train on all sides. Over and under and around and through.

Engineer Barry eased off the throttle, and his engine and tender crept out over the abyss, drawing them all slowly behind. Slowly, cautiously. . . .

"We can only go four miles an hour," Papa explained, "or else it sets the trestle to swaying."

Their passenger coach crawled out next, off of solid land and onto a bridge no wider than the train. Maggie looked down. Flames danced and pranced on the wooden framework of the bridge, up one spar, down another. Hot winds harassed them, shrieking and screeching, the furious voice of the demon. Cinders and embers fell out of the smoky billows, faster and faster, pelting down like hailstones. The cars rocked and rattled.

Maggie gripped Papa's arm like it was her only hope. Hoping against hope that the bridge could hold up two engines. And all these people aboard it.

Papa tightened his other arm around her shoulder. Maggie stared down, seeing nothing beneath them but thick whirling, writhing smoke. Darkness enclosed them. Flames shot through the clouds like lightning. Lightning above and below them. Far below in the gorge, an ominous rumble threatened to rise up. "How far down is it, Papa?" she whispered.

"One hundred and fifty feet," said Papa. "Don't look down. You'll get dizzy."

But Maggie's eyes were riveted. Swirling clouds made it seem as if the trestle was swaying. Maybe it was. It felt like the earth itself was swaying.

It was like looking into hell.

Wrenching her eyes away, Maggie forced herself to look ahead. How far? How much farther? Smoky nothingness lay ahead. It was endless. Earth had dissolved, disappeared. Time dissolved too. Time became eternity. Were they moving at all? Was something holding them back? Could the demon fire do that? Were they in its grip? Maggie remembered with a jolt that this canyon was called Hell's Gate. Icy cold shivers rattled down her spine even as sweat ran from every pore on her body, making her clothes steam. It was all so unworldly. Had real demons come up out of Hell's Gate? Was this the end of the world?

She sagged against Papa, leaning into his solid strength. He tightened his grip around her. The wheels, thought Maggie. Listen to the wheels. Look, they're real, they're moving. Maggie couldn't tell earth from space, but she could see the wheels and hear their muffled rasp of steel on steel. The train had to be moving too. Maggie gripped the handrailing with both hands and Papa held her tightly. Don't look down. Look ahead.

Small flickering fires poked through the smoke. Staying put, not cavorting through clouds. Constant. Little brush fires? But where? She strained to see through the smoke. There, up ahead. And rocks! Solid rocks, staying put like they were stacked, like a wall.

"There's the canyon wall," said Papa, his breath a gasp of relief. "We're almost there!"

Yes, Maggie saw, the rocks formed the rim of the gorge. The support beams that braced the cross-beamed trestle were bolted to steel anchors embedded into the solid rock canyon walls, mere feet away. Maggie scanned the canyon wall to locate the fires she had seen and nearly stopped breathing.

The trestle braces were on fire. The wooden support beams and timbers braced against the gorge wall burned fiercely, all along their length. Slowly the train eased toward those flaming timbers, still barely crawling along. Maggie sucked in a choking lungful of smoke, eyes darting from canyon wall to burning spars to canyon wall, coughing and choking at the same time.

Whistle hoots erupted from the lead engine. Maggie's head jerked up and she peered forward. The first engine was across! Then the tender and then their passenger coach. On solid ground. Beneath her now were ties and rails and the gravel roadbed. She tossed her head back and let out a whoop. Papa pulled her back into the vestibule.

"Take some deep breaths," he said, arms on her shoulder, voice still full of worry.

Maggie gulped down a couple of breaths, then stared up into Papa's grave face, realizing they were not yet out of danger. Nine cars and another engine followed them, still out on the trestle—on a burning trestle, not designed or built for this weight, this stress. If it gave under the last engine, the entire train would be dragged back. They would all be hurtled into that cauldron of fire and lightning and smoke and whirlwind. Papa pulled her into his arms and they waited. Waited.

Engineer Best loosed a long, long triumphant whistle

blast from his rear engine, and Engineer Barry sounded an answering blast. Wheet! Wheet! Wheet! Wheet! A jarring pull rocked the train as the powerful locomotives opened their throttles and released their brakes. They were all across!

Great steel wheels clanked in rhythm against the steel rails, louder and faster and prouder. Whistles rang repeatedly. Coal smoke billowed out of smokestacks, leaving behind the angry howl of the raging fires.

Maggie leaned against Papa's strong chest. He breathed a deep, deep sigh, smiled down at her, brushed back her sooty hair, and kissed her forehead.

Sudden roaring—splintering—screeching crashes rose up behind them. A scream of twisted steel and splitting timbers. Maggie screamed too, terror in her eyes and her heart and her voice. Deafening crashes reverberated and echoed through the canyon, squeals and screeches careening against sandstone and steel. Maggie couldn't stop screaming, locking both hands around the handrail. The demon, furious and frustrated by their escape, must be flailing his way up from hell itself!

"It's the trestle, Maggie, the trestle," Papa shouted at her, shaking her shoulders. "The trestle burned through and crashed down into the canyon, into the Kettle River. But we're across. We're safe." His firm, steady voice and his touch reached through Maggie's panic and her screams quieted to sobs. "We're safe," Papa repeated.

He stepped down onto the metal step and looked back. "The folks in Sandstone refused to come aboard—they couldn't see the danger. Now the river is their only hope."

Maggie collected her wits and concentrated on calming her breathing. Hand over her heart, she felt its frantic beat begin to slow. She looked up at Papa, but his eyes were riveted back to Sandstone. He'd said, "The river is their only hope . . . "

Suddenly her thoughts rocketed back to Jack and Eddie. Perhaps they were stranded in Hinckley, with no hope of escape. If they missed the Limited, they had no hope at all. Her heart raced again, as though outrunning the persistent demon.

The engines raced on, pulling ahead of the raging inferno. The firestorm had neither stopped nor lessened. They had only outrun it. It still chased them. Unleashed and unharnessed, the demon relentlessly pursued them.

Maggie and Papa stared back from the platform. Pictures burst into Maggie's mind of the buildings of Hinckley bursting into flames, of people running for their lives, clothes on fire, dropping in the streets. Crying and yelling and screaming. Where were they now?

Where were Jack and Eddie?

"You should never have brought us here, Papa," Maggie whispered, not realizing she was speaking aloud.

But Papa heard her. His hand released its grip on the rail, and he put it over his eyes, his head bowed. He swayed for an instant, then leaned against the wall of the coach. A tremor ran through his body.

Maggie never noticed. She stared back into rumbling black smoke that flashed angry lightning eyes at the fleeing train. Had the demon devoured her brothers?

BRIEF RESPITE
Evening, September 1, 1894

Papa entered the darkened coach. Oil lamps flickered weakly through the haze of smoke that layered the air. Ragged moans rippled through the crush of burned and traumatized refugees. Voices murmured fervent prayers, pleaded for the lost and the missing.

"Superior, next stop," called Papa. "We'll stop only long enough to switch engines and let off anyone who wants to stay here, then we'll go on to Duluth." A few weary heads turned his way, too exhausted to shout questions. "We wired ahead at the brief stop in Partridge," he continued. "The folks in Duluth know we're coming and will have lodging, food, and medical help available."

Like a wounded bird, a long sigh fluttered up from Maggie's breast. Superior. Clean, fresh air, damp and cool from the lake. She wanted never to leave again.

As the train pulled into the Superior station, Maggie, again in her seat by Gramma, stared out the coach window. But she didn't see the engineers and brakemen being led away, burned and nearly blinded from exposure to heat and flames and cinders. She saw herself on her last day in Superior, on this very platform. They never should have left. But Papa hadn't listened. Neither had Gramma. Nor Jack and Eddie. Now everything they owned was destroyed, and Jack and Eddie were missing. Maggie rubbed her forehead. She had a terrible headache. Replacement engineers shuttled the train on toward its final destination.

"Duluth. Last stop," called Papa. Maggie became aware of lights ahead. Many lights. Streetlights, carriage lights, lamps, and lanterns. And throngs of people. As the dazed refugees staggered off the train, Duluth citizens shepherded them into the depot, police directing the milling crowds. When Papa finished his duties, he and Maggie and Gramma stood together on the platform. A towering policeman approached them.

"There's coffee and sandwiches inside, folks," he said, "or we can take you to one of the cafes for a hot meal. The Armory and churches have places for you to sleep."

"We need water," croaked Gramma. "A restroom." Maggie glanced at her. Gramma's white hair was ashy gray. So was her face.

"We'll want something to eat and drink," said Papa, "but quickly. We want to get over to the St. Paul-

Duluth station. Has the Limited arrived there yet?"

"You're the first refugees to reach Duluth," the officer said. "I heard some people got through south to Pine City. Come have a quick sandwich, and I'll take you over to the other station."

"I'll come too, if I may." Dr. Stephan had joined them. "I'm told there's a relief train being organized to go back to Hinckley, and they need doctors."

"We'll help you too, Dr. Stephan," said Gramma, "once we find Jack and Eddie."

Maggie nearly choked. Hinckley was the last place in the world she wanted to go! What was Gramma thinking? Maggie's headache got worse. Worse than terrible.

But . . . Jack and Eddie. Jack and Eddie. What if they were hurt, needing help? Through her mind flashed pictures of desperate, running people, their hands reached out to beg for help. What if Jack had done that? Asked for help—asked to be saved? What if Eddie were hurt, reaching out for her? How could she refuse? Maggie shook her head, trying to erase the mental images.

She'd have to go back. Swallow her terror and find her brothers.

At the St. Paul-Duluth station, Papa's uniform drew attention. The yardmaster came over and shook his hand. "I'm Dave Williams. Did you folks come in on the rescue train?"

"Yes, sir," said Papa. "I'm Conductor Jules Grant. What news of the Limited? I'm hoping my two sons would be aboard."

A frown drew down Mr. Williams's handlebar mustache, and he shook his head slowly from side to side. A sharp stabbing pain cramped Maggie's midsection, and she drew her arms tight across her chest.

"First reports indicated that it burned up," said Mr. Williams. "Later reports said there were survivors, but they were in dire need. I wired down to Conductor Roper at Willow River. The fire ran south and east of his station, which escaped undamaged. I told him to take his way-freight—to try to reach the Limited and bring back any survivors." He took off his cap and ran a kerchief across his sweaty brow. "Also, we'll soon have a relief train leaving from here."

Dr. Stephan reached out and gripped his arm. "I'm a doctor. I intend to go along on your relief train."

"All of us do," Papa added.

Mr. Williams looked at Maggie and Gramma, alarm all over his face. "Not the women."

"We need to find my grandsons," said Gramma, determination back in her voice and manner. "And there'll be folks that need nursing."

"It's not that," said Mr. Williams. He turned to Dr. Stephan. "The fires seem to have died down—the winds calmed down some toward evening, and, when the fire reached cut-over lands at the Wisconsin border, we think it just sort of quit. But you're still going into a dangerous situation. There's plenty of smaller fires still burning." He hesitated, then continued, his voice quieter but still urgent. "You'll see terrible things. Nothing a woman should have to endure."

Maggie thought she had endured plenty already. She had seen more terrible sights than anyone should have to endure.

"We'll all go," Gramma insisted, in a voice that brooked no argument. "Help is needed desperately."

In a very short time, they were all aboard the Short Line, Mr. Williams included. Heading back south.

Maggie hugged her arms across her chest, struggling against an overwhelming feeling of panic. How could that monstrous fire—that red demon—have just quit? They could all die, going back there. And for what?

Dead bodies?

SKUNK LAKE
Night, September 1, 1894

Although going south on a different rail line, one that had so far escaped the forest fire, Maggie could see they were heading into disaster. The farther they went, the denser the smoke, the blacker the sky, punctuated with faraway red flares. Near eleven o'clock, the Short Line drew into Willow River. Everyone scrambled off the train to confer with the stationmaster. Dead ahead on the tracks, a way-freight idled, steam up and hissing.

Maggie jumped off the bottom step, stopped, and stared. Smoky night air swirled dreamily around the depot lights. Like fog. The same way mist off Lake Superior wound itself around the gas streetlights. Like home.

Voices swirled around Maggie's head.

"Conductor Sullivan is inside the depot. He and a few other survivors of the Limited managed to walk up here. Don't know how. They're badly burned."

Foggy voices. Maggie shook her head to clear it

but heard, "They don't hold much hope for any other survivors ... "

Maggie shuddered. She raced into the tiny depot and stopped so suddenly she almost fell forward. Slumped in chairs, crumpled on the floor, leaning against each other, sprawled the refugees from the Limited. Hair and clothes charred, skin blistered, many had wet cloths over their eyes.

Maggie stooped, looked into faces. She stared into every face, face after face, her heart sinking a bit lower each time a stranger stared back. Not Jack. Not Eddie. They weren't here.

Maggie sat back on her heels. They must be farther down the line. She would have to go farther south. She ran out to tell Papa.

Papa just nodded. The stationmaster must have told him.

"Mr. Williams is sending the Short Line straight back to Duluth with these survivors," Papa said. "They need immediate medical help ... "

"But how can we go on?" Maggie blurted out, interrupting Papa.

"We'll go ahead on the way-freight. It'll get us as far as the Short Line could," Papa said, leading her over to the boxcar attached to the stubby engine. He and Dr. Stephan gave Maggie and Gramma a hand up into the boxcar. The stationmaster handed up a wooden crate for Gramma to sit on, then gave each of them a bandanna.

"Tie these over your mouths and noses," he instructed. "It'll be easier to breathe. It's hot as blazes ahead."

Maggie resisted the urge to tell him what "hot as blazes" was really like. Too hot to breathe. Hope leaked out of her like melted butter. Too hot to live through.

Sitting cross-legged on the floor of the boxcar, Maggie stared out the open doorway. Stands of pine still lined the tracks, blackly silhouetted against a brighter sky, swirled through with drifting smoke. The entire night sky unfurled ahead of them, flashing and whirling with red like the aurora borealis. Strong hot breezes swept through the car, swirling up straw and sawdust.

Heat and light intensified as the train steamed into fire-ravaged countryside. Maggie had to inch farther back into the boxcar, the breeze now uncomfortably hot against her face. Still, she watched out the open doorway, her eyes widening, her heart beating faster. Tall tree trunks burned like pillars of fire, a temple to the red demon. Glowing embers undulated across the ground like waves on a lake of molten lava. The sky curved over them like flames inside a furnace. Hell, revisited.

The engineer leaned out his window, depending on the dim engine headlamp to watch the rails ahead for broken or warped tracks, constantly slowing the throttle. Finally, lights glowed ahead.

"Miller Station," said Conductor Roper. The signal light gleamed red. Stop.

A switchman in striped coveralls, his eyes haggard, lifted his lantern. He peered up at the men in the engine.

"The track ahead is impassable," he said. "Ties are all burned through, bridges burned, rails spread apart."

"Got any handcars?" asked Mr. Williams.

The switchman nodded. "Yup."

Maggie touched Papa's arm, looking quizzically up at him. "If it's impassable, how can handcars get through?"

"They're small and light enough that a crew of men can carry them past broken rails or burned bridges," explained Papa. "With handcars, we can keep going."

Everyone transferred aboard five handcars: a repair crew, doctors, Mr. Williams, and Maggie, Papa, and Gramma. Maggie settled back against the fulcrum of the hand-pumping mechanism that pumped like a playground seesaw. Piled around them were stacks of lumber, rails, and tools for the crewmen to repair track and bridges.

Darkness enveloped them as they pulled out of the station, their only light a few lanterns, although Maggie saw scattered fires across the countryside. The pump screeched like fighting tomcats. The metal wheels rasped against the rails and against Maggie's nerves. It got fearfully hot. The smoke grew thicker and thicker.

"Thick enough to cut with a bread knife," Gramma said.

The handcars screeched to a stop.

"Wait here," Papa commanded Maggie. Men on the front car shouted. Shadows danced as their lanterns waved. More shouting, clanks of tool chests, scrapes of timbers drifted back. "There's no danger," said Papa, coming back. "A small bridge burned away. You can come and watch."

Gramma decided to stay put, but Maggie wanted to see it. She walked to the edge of a wide creek bed and looked down. Warped rails sagged over a smoking gulch—it was a much smaller version of the trestle over Kettle River. Maggie returned quickly to Gramma. Her headache had not eased, and now her stomach hurt too. But the sounds of clanging steel and cracking timbers, counterpointed by shouted directions from the section crew foreman, made any relief impossible. Too restless to sit, Maggie walked back to the creek bed to watch.

One crew of men with mauls and crowbars ripped

apart burned timbers. Another crew set new timbers in place, hammering large nails through crossbeams, with the foreman directing their placement. A third crew shoveled and smoothed rough gravel to repair roadbed on each side of the creek. Quickly following them, yet another crew laid new rail over finished sections, pounding spikes into fresh wood ties that they placed on the roadbed, then across the trestle as quickly as the previous crew moved ahead.

Oddly, this furious bustle settled Maggie. Things were being done. A site of destruction was being rebuilt. When the men tossed their equipment and supplies back on the handcars, Maggie felt better, glad to move on. But they soon stopped again.

"Stay there," Papa called back to Maggie, his voice ragged this time. She could hear Papa's and Dr. Stephan's voices drifting back to her through deep darkness. "No way to identify ... burned beyond recognition ... have to leave them here for now ... "

Dr. Stephan tossed a woman's scorched purse on the handcar when he climbed back on. "This might identify them," was all he said. Now Maggie was glad of the darkness as the handcar moved on.

Her eyes smarted and it hurt to rub them. Gramma coughed several times, and Papa dipped a tin cup into the water pail for her, then wet their bandannas.

Maggie wiped her face and eyes, then held the cloth over her mouth and nose. Several times more, the handcars stopped, sometimes to repair tracks, sometimes to inspect bodies. Maggie dreaded Papa coming back, choking out words that he had found Jack or Eddie. But if the bodies were beyond recognition, how could Papa or Dr. Stephan tell?

Gramma had her head in her apron again.

"I'm quite sure it's not the boys," Papa said. He started to cough. Couldn't stop. Dr. Stephan whacked him on the back between his shoulder blades. No one talked. The squeaky pump quieted as they coasted into a large open area—the swamp—surrounded by a circle of burning trees. Everyone climbed off the handcar and stood deathly still, staring.

It looked like a lake, but black, black as a pool of tar. Stretched out for acres, black, with a smoke or a mist or will-o'-the-wisp hovering over it, slithering across the black water. Maggie put her handkerchief over her nose, it stunk so. Like dead fish, or dead birds, or dead frogs. Like things burned to death. She glanced around—no bodies within her sight, but she didn't want to look closer.

"Skunk Lake," whispered Mr. Williams. "Just a slough, really." His voice hovered too, swallowed up in the black mist. Still-burning tree trunks crackled, their light flickering through the ground fog, darting through like snakes. "Look yonder, down the track," his voice echoed. "The Limited."

Without speaking, everyone looked. Everyone walked up to the ruins of the Limited. Its burned-out, blackened metal framework and steel wheels tilted crazily on warped tracks. The cars were separated, as though some had the strength to stagger on, leaving others behind as they died. The coal tender stood a distance ahead, giving off an intense red glow like a giant parlor stove, still hissing, lighting the area around it.

Farther down the track, standing alone, loomed the huge black bulk of the locomotive. Still, not moving. Deathly quiet, no hissing, no crackling. There were no signs of life, no sound, no movement.

"Are they all dead?" whispered Mr. Williams, glancing from the skeletal train to the black spectral swamp.

No one moved or spoke. No one knew what to do. Gramma began to cry softly.

Maggie turned and looked across the swamp called Skunk Lake. Eerie, black, swirling black fog, hiding . . . what? Where were the people who had ridden the train this far? There were no bodies here. The train couldn't have gotten here alone. Unless the people had jumped off, but surely not all of them. Her eyes searched the dimness, looking for signs of life, for forms that were not normal swamp life. How deep was the lake? Sloughs weren't deep. She yelled, "Jack! Eddie!" Again, louder, "Jack! Eddie!"

Startled, the others stared at her, then across the swamp. Raising hands to their mouths, they called too, all at once. "Hello! Hello! Anyone out there?"

From all across the smoky dismal swamp, looming dark figures rose up. Black human shapes lurched through the clinging dark mist toward them, toward the voices. A terrible smell of stagnant water and seared flesh rose too, mingled with acrid smoke. The figures struggled through black water that snagged them with burned swampgrass and weeds, splashing and lunging toward them, arms reaching out, voices calling, "Thank God! Help has arrived! We're saved!" Stumbling, staggering toward hope and help.

Maggie ran down the scorched slope and splashed into murky water and scorched cattails. Her shoes sucked into muddy swamp muck, skirts dragging in stinking mud.

"Jack? Eddie? Where are you?" Desperation propelled her, she fell into stinky black water, rose up and ran again and called again, "Jack! Eddie!"

A soot-caked, mud-covered, stinky creature lumbered toward her. "Maggie?" it croaked. Black arms trembled toward her, reached for her, as he staggered ahead, shrouded in black fog. Breathy gasps of air burbled out of his lungs.

Maggie grabbed him and clutched him close and hugged him and hung on to him. Eddie was alive! Here, and alive! In her arms.

"You came. You found me, little sister," Eddie whispered. He smelled like a roasted frog. He squished like swamp bottom when he hugged her.

Tears streamed down Maggie's face. Eddie was alive. She had found him. He had been waiting for her to come. Papa and Gramma splashed into the water, unmindful of the stink, and wrapped themselves around Eddie and Maggie. No one could talk, just held on to each other.

Finally Maggie raised her wet face from Eddie's chest. "Is Jack here?"

No answer. Maggie felt him trembling, shaking.

Papa's voice quavered. "Was he with you?"

Eddie pulled back a bit, looking from Maggie to Papa. "He wasn't aboard," he whispered hoarsely. "Wasn't he with you?"

Dr. Stephan bounded down into the water, pulling them out and onto the sloping shoreline. He threw a blanket over Eddie's shoulders, hugging him as he did so.

"You're shaking," he said. "Shivering. Cold air

flowed in behind the firestorm. All the survivors are chilled." His voice firmed up as he talked his doctor talk. "Drastic change in temperature and their hours in the swampwater."

No one spoke, numbed not from the cold night air, but from dread. Jack wasn't here; he hadn't been on either train. The only explanation was unthinkable.

Not realizing their fear, Dr. Stephan settled them on blankets on the roadbed that sloped up from the shallow lake, tending to Eddie, urging him to eat the bread, drink the milk he offered. After seeing Eddie had no serious burns, Dr. Stephan left to tend other survivors.

Eddie gazed across the scorched remains of Skunk Lake, the cup in his hand trembling. "A lot of people came to the depot wanting to get out on the Limited," he said, a quiet urgency to his voice, needing to tell what he knew. "It was due to arrive in about fifteen minutes. Jack and his buddies ran around among them. Some folks came inside out of the wind and smoke, but most of us stood outside watching the fire approach. Closer and closer. Faster and faster." He took a shuddering breath, then another.

"Tom stayed in the office, telegraphing nearby stations, trying to contact the Limited, trying to warn other towns about the fire and how fast it was coming."

Maggie reached for Eddie's hand, held it tightly to

stop its shaking. And to stop her own hand's trembling.

"Someone yelled, 'Everybody out! The roof is on fire!' We looked up. The roof had burst into flames, in seconds." Eddie turned to look at Papa, sitting on the ground beside him with his arms crossed over his knees. "About then, we heard the whistle from your engine at the Eastern Minnesota Railway Depot, and most folks took off running across town to try and catch it."

Papa's head went down into his arms.

"I didn't see Jack again," whispered Eddie. "I figured he escaped on your train."

THE LIMITED
Late night, September 1, 1894

"Come, help me get the engineer down," echoed a dis-
embodied voice drifting through smoke. Searching to
see where, or who, the speaker was, Maggie glimpsed
Dr. Stephan silhouetted against the huge black locomotive, orange shapes and shadows flickering across his
face and the charcoal iron mass behind him. Shaking off
a spooky shiver, she raced with the others to help.

Eddie climbed up into the cab, his arms grasping
the semiconscious engineer. Papa reached up for the
man's legs.

"It's Jim Root," said Eddie, as they lowered him to
the ground. Maggie knelt beside the wounded engineer, supporting his head on her lap as Dr. Stephan
inspected his burns. Tearing her apron into strips,
Gramma dipped them in a water pail, wrung them out,
and handed Maggie the bandages. Maggie gently
swabbed Jim's burned face and eyes, biting her lip.
There was a lot of blood, a lot of cuts on his face.

"From broken glass," said Eddie, watching her.

Dr. Stephan lifted Jim's head and wrapped a clean gauze bandage around his forehead and neck. Maggie held the wet cloth in place over his burned eyes.

"It's better now," she whispered gently, "you'll be all right."

Jim had regained consciousness. "It sounds like angels talking," he muttered. "But judging from the way I hurt all over, I must still be alive."

Gramma patted his cheek. "You certainly are." She helped him to sit up and draped a blanket over his shoulders. "Now see you stay that way."

Mr. Williams strode over. "I'm taking the severely injured folks back to Duluth on the handcars. My work crews will stay to repair the tracks and trestles, then we'll come back with the freight train for the rest of the survivors. Will you be all right here?"

"We'll be fine," said Papa. "But after we rest a bit, we'll try to get through to Hinckley. There may be survivors there too."

Mr. Williams started to object but stopped when he saw the determined set of Papa's jaw, evidently realizing Papa had only one of his missing sons with him.

"Good luck to you," he said, shaking Papa's hand. He and Dr. Stephan helped Jim to his feet, supporting him on each side, and led him to a handcar.

Maggie, Papa, and Gramma settled down again with Eddie on the sloping roadbed alongside the engine. Maggie moved close to Eddie for warmth as much as comfort. Eddie wrapped his blanket around both their shoulders.

"Strange how cold the night air became," remarked Gramma, leaning against her son and sharing his blanket. Clouds blotted out the moon and stars, but flaring embers on the ground reflected eerily off their dark surface.

"How did you escape, Eddie?" Papa asked quietly.

Eddie gazed across the smoking smoldering landscape, but Maggie knew he was seeing Hinckley again.

"We tried to put out the fire at the depot, but it was hopeless," Eddie said, his voice trembling. "The heat drove us back. Tom stayed inside at his telegraph. The depot collapsed on him. He never got out."

"Oh, no, no," Maggie whispered, putting her hand over her eyes.

Eddie shook his head as though to shake away the image of the burning depot.

"By then, the entire town was on fire, and your train had left. But I recollected that according to Tom's latest messages, the Limited was still coming. So those of us still there ran north up the tracks to meet it. More people joined us as we ran. Some of them jumped into the river when we crossed the Grindstone River Bridge. I don't think they knew how shallow it is. Others ran into the millpond by the lumberyard, but most of us kept running. There was fire all around us in every direction."

He shook his head again, harder this time. "We ran a mile or more to the top of Big Hinckley Hill. It was clearer there—we'd gotten ahead of the fire. We saw the Limited coming, barreling along at full speed. Jim braked to a stop when he saw us running toward him. He got down from the engine and asked us what was wrong. He hadn't seen any fire yet. Just black smoke." Eddie talked faster, louder. "We told Jim a huge forest fire was chasing after us—had already burned up Hinckley. The winds were so strong they near to blew us away. Just standing there, the oil dripping from the couplings caught fire under the train—it was that hot. Jim hollered for us to climb aboard."

His words tumbling over themselves, Eddie went on. "Two, three hundred people scrambled on while we talked. The coaches were jammed full, people standing in the aisles, crowding the vestibules at the entrances, standing on the steps. Someone even clung to the cow-catcher in front of the engine." Eddie took a deep breath. "Jim soon had the engine going in reverse, wide open. I looked out the window to see how close the fire was following us."

Eddie stopped, frowned, ran both hands through his hair.

"What happened?" Maggie whispered.

"I couldn't believe what I was seeing," Eddie said. "Superhot winds, gusts and gales, twisted the trees and splintered them apart. Suddenly, out of that black writhing sky, dropped a tornado." He stared wide-eyed into their faces. "A huge cyclone of fire, bearing headlong down on our train."

He shuddered, his gaze drifting back off into space. "Such a deafening roar, like when you stand on the platform as a fast freight goes past at full throttle. Then a wave of fire hit us hard, rocking the entire train, shattering all the windows on the west side. I thought we'd be blown right off the tracks." Eddie rocked sideways as if he felt it again. Maggie grabbed his arm and held it tightly.

"The train kept moving, though. Everyone screamed and crowded to the other side of the aisle. Flames whooshed in the broken windows, and we pulled down the rubber shades, but they burned up too. People went crazy. One man jumped out the window into the fire. Another would have followed him if Conductor Sullivan hadn't grabbed him. Some big guy ran down the aisles yelling, 'We'll all go to heaven together!'"

Eddie stopped, gulping in several deep breaths. Maggie reached up and rubbed his back, leaning her head against his shoulder.

"After the wave of fire went by," said Eddie, his voice steadier, "it got a bit better. Porter Blair quieted everyone down, handing out water from the coolers at the end of the coach. He gave a couple of us wet towels and told us to help people who had burns."

The terror of Maggie's own train ride rocked her, panic rising in her throat. She swallowed hard, holding down sobs.

"The train slowed way down," Eddie said. "The fireman, McGowan, told me later that Jim had gotten badly cut when his windows shattered and evidently he had passed out. The throttle shut itself down. McGowan was able to revive Jim with water from the engine tank, and Jim got us moving again. I don't think many passengers even realized what had happened."

He gulped down what sounded to Maggie like a sob. "I had realized we were slowing down and had figured the engineer was . . . out of commission. Sure reckoned we were goners then. Mighty relieved when we picked up speed again."

Eddie looked away, down the tracks at the ruined coaches. "There was plenty to worry about in our coach, anyway. The car was burning—the roof was on fire and flames licked in through the transom. Thick smoke poured in through the windows, and the curtains and upholstery started to burn. We beat out those fires with wet towels. Some people's clothes caught on fire. We beat those flames out with wet towels too."

A choking sob escaped Maggie's throat. She hadn't had to face anything that bad.

"All of a sudden," Eddie said, "the train braked to a screeching halt, then reversed several feet. When we looked out, we saw water alongside the tracks! Someone yelled, 'Skunk Lake!' and people shoved and scrambled out of the coaches toward that water. Porter Blair stayed calm, getting people out without their stampeding over each other. He handed me a bucket of water to throw on the doorway and steps, because people's clothes caught on fire as they jumped through and down."

Maggie shut her eyes tight, trying to shut out the images of Eddie struggling against such horrific fires.

Eddie kept right on. "Hundreds of people ran down the slope to the lake, breaking through a barbed-wire fence to splash into the water. Very shallow water. They ran farther, but it never got deeper than a foot or so. Blair and I stayed by the train throwing water on people still getting off. Soaking their burning clothes. Everything around us burned. The train, the ground, the air itself, it seemed."

Eddie sat straight up, his voice strident again. "We had to get to the water. But McGowan yelled at us to get Engineer Root into the lake, so we raced to the engine. Jim couldn't see. He was too weak to walk. We hauled him down into the water and sank down beside him. The so-called lake was only about eighteen inches deep—just a slough! We soaked our coats in swamp water and covered our heads. Fiery debris dropped all over us. Everywhere."

Eddie stopped talking, gasping in breaths of air. Gramma gave him more water and Papa patted his back. Tears ran down Maggie's face as she held onto Eddie's arm. But Eddie wasn't finished. He rubbed his arm across his face, brushing away tears and soot.

"Then another wave of flames swept over us. Another deafening roar, like steady thunder. Sheets of fire flapped over us. Raced around us like it was trying to suck us up out of the slough. We lay down in the water, coming up for a breath of air when we had to, but it was superheated. It smelled and tasted like poison."

Looking around the slough, Eddie said, "After it passed over, I looked up. All around the shore, the trees burned. A huge circle—a burning wall of trees—surrounded us."

Maggie looked around at the still-smoldering tree trunks, seeing it all as Eddie described it.

"Three waves of fire went over us," Eddie said quietly. "It happened three times." He turned and looked over his shoulder up the slope, as if to make sure nothing else was coming.

"After that," he went on, "it burned itself out, mostly, but we stayed in the water till it seemed safe to come out. The air got cold, like after a thunderstorm, and we got chilled. Jim Root said his legs were cold and numb and he wanted to go back to his engine. The coal in the tender was still burning awfully hot, so McGowan and I uncoupled the engine and pushed it down the track a ways before we carried Jim to his cab. He seemed more comfortable on the warm floor."

With a sigh that seemed to come up from his boots, Eddie looked out over the slough. Survivors huddled in little groups around its edge, draped with blankets.

"But the strangest thing . . . ," he said, his voice quiet and bemused. "The fires had finally burned down but were still bright enough so that it wasn't ever completely dark. Then, crazily, all these dark ashes fell out of the sky, floating down like snowflakes. Black snowflakes. It was like another world. Dark, with flickering red light. Soft, gentle, dark snowflakes. Eerily beautiful."

Maggie saw it in her mind's eye, but it wasn't beautiful. It was the red demon, catching his breath.

NOT JACK. NOT JACK.
Just after midnight, September 2, 1894

"Lights! Down the track. They're coming from Hinckley!"

Maggie jumped up, confused and disoriented. Where was she? What was happening? A frightened gasp drew smoky air into her lungs and she coughed. Skunk Lake. They were at Skunk Lake. She had fallen asleep on the ground.

Lantern lights bobbed down the tracks, and Maggie heard the squeal of pumping handcars coming from the direction of Hinckley. It was still night, with its strange ember-lit darkness.

"Now we can get through to Hinckley," called Papa over his shoulder as he ran to meet the rescuers. Dazed survivors roused themselves and staggered forward as a row of handcars joined together by long planks stopped close to the disabled engine.

"We sure are glad to see you folks walking about!" the rescuers said. "We gave up hope of finding anyone alive and breathing. Climb aboard, we'll take you to Pine City." Forty or so survivors clambered on. The rest settled down again alongside the slough.

Maggie jumped on the lead car as Papa and Eddie gave Gramma a lift up. Settling her skirts, Gramma asked, "Why aren't the others coming?"

"They're waiting for the relief train to come back from Duluth," explained Papa. "They don't see much point in going to Hinckley."

"Hinckley's pretty much destroyed," said one of the workmen between pulls on the pumping mechanism. "But we can take you down the line to Pine City. The fire missed us there, so we can give you food and shelter."

All Maggie heard was "pretty much destroyed . . ." Her heart lurched. What of Jack? What had happened to Jack?

"We need to get to Hinckley," Maggie heard Papa say. "I need to find my son. Are there survivors in Hinckley?"

She held her breath. Could anyone have survived?

"A few folks dove into the water in the gravel pit," said the workman. He exchanged glances with his partner across the handpump. "Most folks perished."

"Jack knew about the gravel pit!" said Maggie. "He would have gone to the gravel pit." Lost in thought, she didn't hear anyone answer her. She must find Jack at the gravel pit. That's where she would go.

Sitting as close to the center of the car as she could, Maggie averted her eyes from the sides of the tracks, where charred black bodies sprawled alongside the rails. A lot of people had missed the train or had fallen off. She began to worry about what she would see in Hinckley. Surely there would be bodies, an awful lot of bodies. All the bodies of the people who she'd seen from her train window, running toward the train, too late to catch it. Dear God, Jack may have been one of those people! But no, no, he'd gone to the gravel pit. She forced her mental images to Jack, splashing into the water, to safety.

Time distorted itself, making the ride seem endless. Maggie thought she would lose her mind if she didn't get to Hinckley soon. She needed to find Jack. She would find him.

Papa squeezed himself down beside Gramma, holding her steady. Gramma's breathing was getting ragged again. Maggie quickly dipped her bandanna in a water bucket and wrung it out.

"Here, Gramma. Put this over your face. Breathe slowly."

Gramma obeyed without comment, and soon her breathing slowed, became less labored. Tenseness eased out of her face, and her color looked better. Relieved,

Maggie's stomachache eased ever so slightly.

Finally their small procession came over Big Hinckley Hill. Smoke and heated air drifted up to greet them. Maggie stood on the handcar, trying to see the town. Though still the middle of the night, the slight valley was thoroughly lit by still-burning buildings, the fires gleeful, celebratory. Great piles of red embers danced and flickered. The crackling flames sounded like haughty laughter. The demon hadn't left.

The handcars stopped just north of the Grindstone River. Nothing was left of the bridge but sagging, twisted rails loosely spanning a smoky gap. Everyone got off and stood at the edge of the riverbank, staring speechless into the town, an open-pit furnace that had devoured most of its fuel. Maggie gazed east to west, looking for buildings still standing, for a pond of water that would be the gravel pit. Smoke drifted across the town, whirling in little eddylike whirlpools, waves of red embers distorted by swirling columns of heated air. She'd have to walk into the waiting room of hell.

The rescue crew decided to haul the handcars across the river manually. Four or six men each grabbed a corner of the car, hoisted, and carried it several feet down the riverbank. They'd rest a minute, then progress another few feet. It was slow work, but the men insisted they could drag it across the shallow river. They urged the doctors and the survivors to walk ahead into Hinckley.

Stumbling and sliding down the riverbank, Maggie and Gramma lifted their long skirts to wade across, but the water scarcely came up to their knees. Nearly stumbling on wet submerged rocks, Maggie glanced upstream, looking for a better place to cross.

She stopped and stared. Black bodies floated down the river toward her. Some hung up on rocks. They didn't look like people—grotesque, twisted, like they still writhed in agony. Maggie felt light-headed, her sight dimming again. She wouldn't faint! She needed to find Jack. She stopped, took several deep, deep breaths.

Already climbing the opposite bank, Eddie said, "Sit down on the rocks, Maggie and Gramma. Your skirts will trail in the coals and ashes. Let me cut them."

His jackknife quickly slashed through the fabric several inches above the hems. Gramma never said a word as a row of hand-tatted lace, scorched and wet, dropped to the ashy ground. Hurriedly they caught up to Dr. Stephan and the others.

At the Brennan Lumber Mill, huge stacks of lumber still burned fiercely, giving off terrific heat. Its brightness revealed bodies along the river's edge, near the millpond, like a trail of bodies trying still to reach the water.

Maggie walked closely behind Papa and Gramma, holding Eddie's arm, praying that Jack had run for the gravel pit and not the millpond.

"There's the main office," said Eddie, pointing to a crumbled chimney and a glowing pile of coals.

Maggie stared, remembering that last despairing whistle blast. The orphan had lived there. Had died there. A tear trickled down her cheek.

"The heat from the lumber must have been tremendous," said Papa. "And the Grindstone River was too shallow to save anyone."

"But the gravel pit was deeper," Maggie said, her voice shaking. "And farther away from the lumberyard."

Papa didn't answer. He stood looking at all the bodies, at the burned remains of a woman with her arms still around two children. Gramma cried softly.

"And the gravel pit was lower than the rest of the town. More protected from the wind," Maggie insisted. "It wasn't close to burning lumber stacks, or buildings, or trees . . ."

Not Jack, she prayed. Not Jack.

Dr. Stephan came back to them and took Gramma by the arm. Papa had her other arm.

"Come along, Alma," Dr. Stephan said. "There will be people who need our help."

They reached Eddie's burned-out St. Paul-Duluth

Depot. Rails broken by the intense heat had twisted into writhing, snakelike forms. The ties were smoldering ashes. Eddie started shaking. Planks and beams stuck up from the burning ruins, crackling and snapping. It wasn't hard to see where the ticket office had been. Where the telegraph had been. Neither Eddie nor Maggie could move. Papa and Dr. Stephan stood beside them. Gramma too. No one said anything. Everyone wiped their eyes. Breaths were shallow, broken by coughs and clearing of throats.

Repairmen worked on the tracks, removing the twisted rails, cussing as the heat burned through their leather gloves. One of them, grimy with sweat and soot, came over.

"Where'd you folks come from?" he asked.

"Where are the people who lived through the fire?" Maggie demanded. "Where are the survivors?"

"We just arrived from Pine City to repair track so the rescue and relief trains can get here," said the workman. "But I heard there's some people in the round-house." He pointed across the smoking landscape. "It's the only building still standing—that and the water tower." He frowned at Papa and Dr. Stephan and Eddie. "There's lots of bodies between here and there. I don't think you want to go any farther."

Maggie looked east to Papa's railroad yards. The

roundhouse stood starkly silhouetted against a few trees burning leisurely at the edge of town. Jack would be there. Jack must be there. Walking away from the depot, their shoes made crunching sounds on the coals and cinders. Dry heat crept up Maggie's legs, snagged around her ankles.

Jack would be there. Maggie determined to block out everything else, the sights and the sounds and the smells, and focus on Jack.

She would find him.

SWIRLING SMOKE
After midnight, September 2, 1894

Gramma hesitated, her hand over her heart. Maggie brushed past her, rushing into the darkened interior of the roundhouse. A sense of space, of high cobwebbed ceilings, and an oily smell of tools and machinery surrounded her, quickly overwhelmed by the odor of charred wood. Faint light filtered through high smoked-over windows, groans and ragged breathing were the only sounds. Maggie discerned forms, crowded and contorted, lying on the floor. Which one was Jack?

Papa stepped in behind her holding a lantern aloft. Muttering, the forms turned over and away. A few sat up, dazed and confused.

Maggie stepped into the maze, searching for a child's body, for Jack, in every face and form. For his cap, his jacket.

"Jack! Where are you?" she demanded. She moved between the shifting forms, soot-covered, red-eyed, their lips swollen and cracked. A shudder ran through her at the sight of their blistered and weeping burns.

"Jack! Wake up. Where are you?" she called, her voice cracking. He had to be here!

Papa touched her shoulder. "He's not here, Missy," he whispered. "Come outside."

Maggie jerked away, ran to a dark corner where a few people huddled in a formless heap. Kneeling down, she grabbed an arm and pulled a person to his feet.

It was a small person. It wasn't Jack. Searching behind every box and crate, Maggie looked into every face, again and again.

Jack was not there. He wasn't there.

Papa stood by the door, his lantern light illuminating deep creases in his brow. Maggie staggered past him, outside to the back of the building, leaning against it for support. Vaguely she heard Papa's voice inside, questioning survivors. She slid down to a sitting position, her back against the warm wood walls. Her throat tightened and tears ran down her face. Where else could she look? Where else could Jack be?

Where else? Smoke drifted past on a now-gentle breeze and clung to her. Through tear-blurred eyes, she sat on her isolated island, Hinckley's single remaining building, and gazed across the simmering, undulating sea of crackling embers hugged by black smoke and heat waves. The fiery sea that embraced so much terror, so much death. Was Jack out there? How could she bear to search the streets?

Something moved. Coming toward her. Too big, too wide to be a person. An animal? A horse or a cow? Wiping her eyes, Maggie sat straight up, peering through wavering smoky air. A cow! Two cows? A cow and a person. A cow and a small person. Something else, too—something smaller. A dog? A cow and a person and a dog?

"Jack!" she yelled, jumping to her feet, running, stumbling, nearly sprawling. She caught herself and ran. Through smoke that snatched at her, through coals that tripped her, she ran.

"Jack! Jack!" It had to be Jack. Dear God, let it be Jack!

The figures stopped, their substance blurred by a drift of dark smoke, obscured by black clouds. The image disappeared. Was it real? Or just swirling smoke? Maggie's heart thudded. Had she imagined it? No! No! She ran toward the smoke, into its thick consuming darkness.

"Maggie!" Jack's heartrending cry nearly made her lose consciousness.

He crashed full-tilt into her arms, crying, shaking, and shuddering. Maggie grabbed him, hugged him, hugged him, hugged him. Unable to talk, she sobbed.

He held on to her as if he would never let go. They cried and sobbed and hiccuped and then laughed for joy. Maggie was vaguely aware of a big, shaggy, smelly, wet dog bounding around them, barking raucously.

Jack was alive! Thank God! And she had found him. Hoped and prayed and searched—and found him. She had stood on the threshold of hell and found her brothers.

After a few moments, Jack stepped back looking up at Maggie with round white eyes rimmed with black soot. "Are the rest . . . ? Are you alone?" he asked. His voice cracked, the words choking him.

Maggie brushed away her tears and grabbed his hand. "Come and see, you little raccoon." She pulled him along to the roundhouse, nearly tripping over the dog that seemed almost physically attached to Jack.

"Papa!" she yelled. Dizzy and giddy, they careened smack into Papa and Gramma and Eddie coming toward them. Arms tangled around each other. Maggie, smushed in the middle, laughed and cried and hiccuped all over again. The dog shoved his big nose into the pile and licked Maggie's face, like he was part of the family. Absent-mindedly, Maggie pulled her arm around his shaggy neck and scooped him into the group hug, where he tried to lick everyone within tongue's reach.

Dr. Stephan, with another young man and woman, ran up, hugging and slapping backs and shaking hands.

After a moment, everyone stepped back to take a breath and grin at each other.

"Pastor! Mrs. Knudsen!" Gramma squealed. "Praise God! You're alive!" Another round of hugging and talking and barking broke out.

Maggie wiped her sleeve across her eyes. It was hard to see everyone. No wonder. They all had black faces— soot and smoke caked on with sweat. White eyes and white teeth shone through the dirt, tear streaks channeled down their cheeks. Clothes were torn, disheveled, scorched.

They looked terrible.

They looked wonderful. Even the incredibly happy, wet, and smelly dog sitting on his haunches with a big dog-smile on his furry face.

Dr. Stephan checked them all over. "Not too badly burned, I'm glad to see. Mostly sore eyes and sore lungs."

"The cow!" remembered Jack, running to fetch the animal he'd left standing in the street, the dog bounding along right on his heels. The cow hadn't gone anywhere. There was nowhere to go.

"I thought we could milk her," Jack said, leading her back, the dog now making an effort to look like he was herding the cow, darting from one side of her to the other.

"Good idea," said Eddie, patting the dog like he was family. "I'll get water buckets from the roundhouse. You milk the cow and I'll draw water from the water tower." He ran off after buckets.

"Now then," said Dr. Stephan, "Jules, you and Pastor need to find food."

Maggie looked across the burning rubble of the town, and her heart sank, joy seeping away. Where on earth, on this scorched earth, could food be found? The milk and sandwiches they had brought from Duluth were long gone. There was nothing left here.

"If I can find where our home was," said Papa, "I can locate the garden. Potatoes and carrots may be edible, under the ground. Probably cooked too."

Pastor Knudsen nodded. "We'll find something." Together they walked into town, picking their way around burning and smoldering piles of rubble.

"Alma, are you up to helping me care for the burned and wounded?" asked Dr. Stephan, giving Gramma an appraising glance. Gramma took a deep satisfied breath of air, coughed a bit, and straightened her smudged eyeglasses.

"Of course," she insisted. "That's what I came for." Eddie returned with buckets and again Gramma wrapped her arms around her two grandsons. "Actually, the second thing I came for."

Jack held the cow, while Mrs. Knudsen milked. Maggie patted the dog, keeping it out of the way while streams of milk splashed into the galvanized railroad pail. Squirt, splash, squirt, splash. Mesmerized by the milky streams, Maggie heard Jack admire Mrs. Knudsen's technique. Maggie savored the normal, everyday sounds, the sweet smell of fresh warm milk, the damp warmth of dog breath on her cheek.

They were alive. Alive and unhurt. They had faced the demon and had survived.

With a distant crash of burning timbers and a shower of sparks as still-burning buildings and beams fell in on themselves, the demon reminded them he still lurked.

With an effort, Maggie focused on the small normal sights and sounds and smells and actions. Tonight people here needed care and comfort. Many would not find their loved ones.

She refused to think of what dawn light might reveal.

THE GRAVEL PIT
Before dawn, September 2, 1894

Unable to sleep, Maggie and Jack walked to the gravel pit, Jack's dog closely following. The eastern sky was barely tinged with light. Maggie sat on a small metal trunk abandoned at the edge of the pond, Jack on the ground leaning back against its side, the dog leaning into Jack.

Maggie looked around the pond—abandoned trunks were scattered all around it and the road running alongside it.

"Why so many trunks here?" she asked Jack. "There must be a hundred or more."

"Everyone just dropped them so they could run faster," said Jack. "Just left all their stuff and ran for their lives." He pushed his hand into his pocket and pulled out his jackknife, opened it and pegged it into the ground.

Looking through dim light and mingling shadows to the main street, Maggie made out still forms sprawled

grotesquely across unrecognizable streets. Had those
been all the people she had seen running toward the
train? A shiver snaked down her back, and she looked
back across the dark water. Scarcely a ripple on it,
though debris floated aimlessly. The surface reflected a
line of burning telegraph poles that traced the path of
railroad tracks. It was eerily quiet too, just the everlasting crackling sounds. And the sound of Jack's knife,
pegging into the ground again and again.

"Look across," said Jack. "See the animals?"

The dog sat up, ears pricked. Maggie saw two horses
on the far side, heads down. Occasionally, one would
swish its tail. A cow, not theirs, stood near them in shallow water, mooing mournfully. A wet bedraggled dog
trotted near, stopped and shook itself. Jack's dog ran
over to it.

Jack, still pegging his knife into the ground, wasn't
looking anywhere except at his imaginary target in the
blackened dirt.

"A lot of animals came in with us . . . ," he said.

"Is that where you found your dog?" Maggie asked,
watching the two stray dogs lick each other's face,
seeming to comfort each other.

"No, before that," said Jack. He folded his knife and
pocketed it. "When the fire first got close, me and Will
and Tony went to Eddie's depot. Lots of people there,

all wanting to get out on the train, I guess. The Limited hadn't arrived yet. Then everything got real bad all of a sudden." Jack's voice got a bit louder, a bit faster. "The fires just whooshed into town—one big sheet of flame landed right on top of the depot roof. All the folks inside rushed out screaming and yelling."

Jack looked over toward the still-burning ruins of Eddie's depot as if he expected the Limited might still arrive. "I tried to find Eddie but couldn't see him anywhere. Tony saw his family go by on a wagon and went with them, north on the Government Road. Will ran on home."

"You couldn't find Eddie?" asked Maggie, trying to keep her voice calm. Jack seemed to be getting antsy, and Maggie didn't want to upset him. She slid down next to him. Maybe she shouldn't ask him any more questions.

The dog trotted back to Jack and sat, his furry bulk tipping Jack into Maggie's side. Maggie put her arm over Jack's shoulder, and he tipped against her, all three of them leaning against the warm, rough, sturdy trunk.

"No, I didn't know if he was still inside the depot, or if he hadn't been there at all, or if he had run off with the others. He didn't know I had been outside— wouldn't have known to look for me." He took a quick deep breath, steadied his shoulders, and went on. "I should have gotten there sooner. Gone inside and found Eddie. My fault I was alone."

"No," said Maggie. "It's no one's fault. Everyone in town was caught and lost and didn't know where to go. How could anyone know a fire could come so fast and be so big and strong? The fire trapped everyone."

Jack sat quietly a second or two, thinking about that. "I suppose so," he shrugged, then went on. "Since I couldn't find Eddie, I ran toward Papa's depot too. The wind pushed me something fierce as I ran up the street past the Morrison Hotel. It was terrible hot. So much smoke in the air it hurt all down my chest when I'd breathe. People ran in every direction, like no one knew where to go. I didn't hear any more train whistles. I figured the train had already left, but I ran toward the depot anyway."

Hearing this, Maggie choked. She couldn't breathe. Jack had been running down the street when her train pulled out! He had been one of the people in the street! She opened her mouth and tried to suck air in, but her throat had tightened shut. She hit her chest, gasping in a breath. Jack sat up on his knees and whacked her back. The dog licked her face, a slobbering dog-drool kiss. After a few gulps of air, she sat back, petting the dog, Jack patting her back.

"Dog's name is Nero," said Jack, his voice back to

normal. He scratched behind the big dog's ears. "He belonged to the neighbor down the street, remember?"

Maggie shook her head. She hadn't paid much attention to neighbors.

"Folks were running down into their root cellars and climbing down wells," said Jack, his voice still conversational. "Nero had crawled under his porch. I called him and he came with me." Jack turned to look at Maggie, pleased he had saved the dog. "Then I wasn't alone anymore."

Maggie started to cry and Jack said, "It worked out just fine, Maggie." Nero started licking her face again.

Pushing the dog's head away, Maggie wiped her face and her eyes. She shouldn't fall apart in front of Jack. She struggled to control herself, telling herself Jack was here, right beside her. He hadn't caught on fire and gotten burned up. She sat back and leaned against the trunk. Jack sat back down too. With a slobbery woof, Nero draped his body over Jack's knees and put his head in Maggie's lap.

Jack's voice started on again, his eyes staring down the street. He pulled himself out from under the dog and pointed into the town as if he recognized where the streets and buildings had been. "Two ladies were kneeling in the street praying, and Angus Hay ran past them and grabbed them and got them up and told them to do their praying in the gravel pit."

Jack's voice squeaked. He turned to look at Maggie, his dark eyes widening. A glimmering point of reflected firelight shone in their centers. "I figured that's where I should go too, so I ran that way. The boardwalks were so hot that pitch oozed out of the planks, and I ran out into the dirt street. All kinds of burning stuff falling out of the sky. My eyes hurt, my lips were dry and stuck together, but I kept running."

Maggie was afraid she'd lose her breath again and, remembering Gramma, made herself breathe slowly. Short ragged gasps were all she could manage. Stay calm for Jack. Let him talk, not fret over her.

Jack stared at the gravel pit. He seemed to forget about Maggie. Maggie followed his glance. The first rays from the rising sun skittered across the dark surface of the pond. The black water lay still and motionless— it looked dead too.

"Finally I stumbled down the bank into the gravel pit and waded out to where it was about three feet deep," Jack said softly. He pointed towards the middle of the pit. "About there, I reckon. Nero came in after me, but didn't come out as deep as me. I wanted to be able to duck under."

Jack was on his knees, quavering a bit like he was standing in water. "Maybe seventy or so folks came here. We kept ducking under the water to keep ourselves wet because burning branches or wood or whatever kept dropping on us. Mr. Hay was there and Chief Craig. And Mayor Webster came with a wagon and some women and children he had rescued. The men splashed water all over us so we wouldn't catch on fire."

Maggie reached over and stroked Jack's hair with her fingers. He leaned against her, sighing. Maggie had found him. He was safe. A quick mental image flashed through her mind of Jack coming home after a baseball game—covered with dirt, grinning, and talking nonstop. "You should have seen me, Maggie, I had a hit with Tony and Will on base. They scored! I won the game! You should have been there." She brushed back his hair and kissed his forehead.

"Wasn't no ordinary fire," said Jack, seemingly lost in his account and oblivious to Maggie's touch. "It roared over us like a freight train. Sounded like one too. It made us all duck under the water. Once I came up and looked toward the lumberyards. I saw a tornado come down! It was fire, all fire, whirling and swirling and sucking up everything. It picked up a whole building—a burning building—and carried it away. Whole stacks of lumber from the yards were sucked up. They caught fire like a bundle of matchsticks and dropped all over town."

Jack's arms were pointing in one direction after another. "There were balls of fire too, big balls, big as washtubs, some bigger. They flew through the sky like baseballs pitched by the devil. Some exploded. Some smashed into buildings and they exploded too. Stores and houses, one after another, just whooshed up in flames."

Jack stared at her, eyes wide, as if he were aware how unbelievable it all sounded. Maggie nodded, letting him know she believed it. She had seen the demon herself.

"I'd duck under the water when a fire wave would go over, come up for a few breaths, and try to see more." Pointing at tilting partial brick walls, he said, "That's the schoolhouse. I watched the roof crash in. Sparks and flames and fire everywhere! And the wind roaring so loud no one could hear anything else."

Maggie stared out over the water, still and dark. It was all over now. The fire had died down. The demon had left. Jack and Eddie were safe. They were all safe.

"We were in the pit about three hours," Jack went on, "then kind of straggled out when we realized the firestorm was over and it was safe to come out. We saw the roundhouse and water tank, so we just sort of wandered over." He stood up, petting his dog. "Nero stuck with me. Guess he's my dog now. The cow followed him out of the pond, so I kept her too. Think we can keep the cow? If no one claims her?"

Maggie had to smile a bit. Jack hadn't forgotten how to use his pleading puppy-dog eyes on her. "It's all right by me," she said. "You going to do the milking?"

"Yeah," said Jack, grinning now. "It's about milking time. Let's go do chores."

Maggie took his hand, and they walked along the tracks back to the roundhouse. The rising sun stretched long shadows behind them, promising a long day ahead.

RELIEF
Morning, September 2, 1894

"Who's that up ahead?" Jack pointed at a figure stumbling toward them. "He can't see. He's rubbing his eyes." Nero watched alertly, a soft rumble in his throat.

Maggie peered through the haze. Another survivor? This one didn't look too good. He was so covered with ashes and cinders he looked completely gray. Probably had bad burns under all those ashes.

"Tony? Tony? Is that you?" called Jack, running to him, Nero trotting behind.

Startled, Maggie followed Jack. Could that be Tony? He was about the right size.

Jack brushed at the boy's clothes, then stopped abruptly when he realized there were holes burned through them and he was brushing burned skin. The boy picked at cinders in the corners of his eyes. He hadn't yet said a word.

"Tony?" Jack asked again.

Maggie pulled out a handkerchief and gently wiped

the boy's eyes. His eyes must have watered, mattering the dust and ashes that had blown into them. Gently she loosened the dried material, like when Gramma unstuck a sty.

"It's coming now," she said softly. "You'll be able to see in a minute."

The boy dropped his hands. Maggie couldn't help but notice all the holes burned in his clothes. He smelled more of smoke than the burning embers around them.

Tony blinked through tears that washed the last of the dirt out his eyes. He looked at Maggie, then at Jack. "Hey, Jack," he said, a tiny smile making creases in his ashy face. Maggie applied her handkerchief to his cheeks. "Sure glad to see you, old buddy." said Tony. "You must have found a safe place somewhere." Tony's face was burned red under the covering of ash. His eyes were puffy, his lips cracked and swollen.

"Are you all right?" asked Jack. He brushed more gently at Tony's jacket. "Looks like you got pretty close to the fire." Nero wagged his tail uncertainly.

Maggie brushed Tony's singed hair with her fingers. He didn't complain of any pain, just looked from Maggie to Jack, kind of dazed.

"Come to the roundhouse with us," she said, taking his hand. She hoped Dr. Stephan would be there.

Near where Eddie's depot had stood, a section crew pulled up and hauled away the twisted tracks, heaping up a stack of black rail mangled every which way. Clangs and clanks and clatters mixed with complaints about gloves burning through. Several people in clean unburned clothes had set a plank across a stack of ties and were handing out food and milk to a group of hungry stragglers. Must be the relief crew from Pine City. Drooling, Nero approached them hopefully. Hungry and thirsty too, Maggie and Tony and Jack joined the line at the plank.

Taking a tin cup of milk, Maggie asked the relief worker, "Do you know Dr. Stephan? Know where he's at?"

Both boys drained their tin cups and held them out for more. Nero sat still, big brown eyes begging. The worker, an older man dressed in striped coveralls, poured milk out of a cream can into a pie plate for Nero and set it on the ground. He glanced over at Tony, at his jacket, and he pushed burned edges away to see Tony's chest.

"I'll find a doctor," he said, heading off toward the roundhouse.

Taking sandwiches and refilled cups from another worker, Maggie and the boys sat on a stack of ties to eat. Nero lapped his plate clean. Tony bit into his sandwich, evidently not feeling any pain.

"Where's your family, Tony?" Maggie asked quietly, remembering that Jack had said Tony had left with them on a wagon heading out of town. Jack, suddenly alarmed, stared at Tony.

Tears trickled down Tony's face. He set his cup down on a tie next to him and roughly wiped his eyes.

"We lost my little sister," he said, terror filling his eyes, replacing the dazed expression. "Fire blocked the road so we left our wagon and ran along the railroad tracks. It got too smoky to even see each other. Somehow we lost my sister." Tears ran down his face, but he didn't seem to notice. No sobs, no cries, just tears. "She was just all of a sudden gone. Couldn't stop and go back for her. Only thing we could see was smoke and fire. Fire everywhere. Had to keep on running."

He looked from Maggie to Jack, blinking to see them. "We heard the train, but we were too far away to catch it. Father yelled to me and my brother to keep running north along the tracks. Said that he would stay with Mother. There was a little swamp there they would go into."

Tony rubbed his eyes with his fists, taking deep breaths that now were almost sobs. "We kept running. Trees fell around us, fire was all over us, but we kept running. I heard lots of screaming behind us, where Mother and Father were. Then I tripped and fell, probably on the rails, and rolled down the side of the tracks. My clothes were burning on my chest. I tried to put out the fire, rolling in sand and gravel. I guess I passed out."

Tony sighed a quavering sigh. Nero whined softly, nuzzling him. "I woke up this morning. Came back to life, like." His voice was softer, lower. "I walked down the track a ways and found my brother's body, burned pretty bad." Tony looked curiously at his hands, as if realizing for the first time they were burned. "But I think he died of suffocation instead of fire. His face looked natural." Nero licked Tony's hands gently. Tony held them out, turning them, as if the dog licks soothed his skin.

Maggie shuddered. Natural! None of this was natural. It was all a horror.

"I went back to the little swamp where my parents stayed," said Tony. He started shaking, his voice too. Jack put his arm around his shoulders.

"There must have been over a hundred people there," said Tony, "all of them burned to a crisp. I sort of wandered around there for a while. I think I found my parents. The shoes looked like Mother's, anyway. . . ." His voice trailed off. He closed his eyes and his head hung low. Jack and Maggie crowded up close to him. Nero pressed in even closer.

"I never found my little sister," Tony whispered. "I don't know about my other sister. Clara, either."

"Clara's safe," said Maggie, grateful she had some good news. "She was on the train with me. She's safe in Duluth."

Jack spoke for the first time, his voice tender. "Your sister will be your family," he said. "A sister is almost like a mother. When I miss my mama too much, I sort of hang around my sister. It'll help, you'll see."

Tony nodded, and Jack lightly slapped his shoulder. Maggie could see the boys understood each other. She said nothing more but looked closely at Jack. She hadn't known he felt that way about Mama and about her. That he needed for her just to be there. He seemed so calm.

Like Mama had been. Mama had taken things as they came, accepting them. Maggie reached over and kissed Jack on the head. He gave her a smile that made her wonder who needed whom. They all walked slowly back to the roundhouse, staying close to the tracks to avoid the shapeless black forms in the streets.

Shriek! A train whistle pierced the dawn. Like it had pierced the smoke and the fire as Papa's train shrieked through flaming forest. Maggie jumped and cried, the escape ride jerking her back, suddenly and fiercely. Nero barked, looking frantically around to see what threatened her.

"Relax, Maggie, you're scaring the dog," Jack said, his voice holding a trace of his old teasing. "It's just a relief train coming in."

Maggie shook her head, embarrassed. She wouldn't do that again—at least, she hoped she wouldn't. They hurried down the track a ways to where the work crew had managed to get new track laid, evidently all the way up from Pine City. Shiny steel rails, spiked straight on new wood ties, stretched back through desolate landscape. Folks gathered in a group around the new track, near to the smoky rubble of the station, eagerly watching the train pull in. Gramma, Papa, Eddie, and Dr. Stephan mingled among them.

The engine screeched to a halt with a whoosh of steam. Several men jumped down from a passenger coach, went immediately to the boxcars, and unloaded supplies—tents, cots, blankets, and crates of food. Gramma bustled right up.

"Good, good, good," she said. "We've been waiting on you. Got a cookstove in there?" she said, peering into the depths of the boxcar.

A portly gentleman in a black suit shook her hand, then Papa's.

"Sir," he said, looking at Papa's sooty uniform and evidently guessing him to be in charge, "we'd be pleased to return the suffering victims to Pine City and

Rush City. Our citizens are anxious to offer their aid."

Papa waved the workers to a cleared area that had once been a railroad yard.

"Set the tents up there. The lady will direct you," he said, indicating Gramma.

Maggie was not surprised. Gramma would have a boardinghouse in a tent set up within an hour. The gentleman cleared his throat and swallowed hard as he looked over the smoking ruins of the town.

"We also offer our services to search for survivors and to help assemble and bury the dead."

Maggie turned away. She didn't want to hear or see anything about that.

Dr. Stephan spoke up. "We'll need lots of help. The bodies have to be interred quickly."

Maggie started to tremble. Papa put an arm around her shoulder, and she sagged against him.

"Hey! Will!" shouted Jack. "Come on, Tony, isn't that Will yonder?" Jack grabbed Tony's hand and raced across crunchy ashes down the street. Maggie turned, startled, ready to call the boys back, but saw another boy through shimmering heat waves, running exhuber- antly toward Jack and Tony, all of them yelling and waving like long lost brothers. Nero bounded along behind, jumping all over them as the boys collided into each other.

"Go along too, Missy," said Papa. "Join the party." Maggie walked hesitantly over to the boys, who were settling themselves on a bare patch of ground, still slapping hands and shoulders. She wasn't sure they'd want a big sister around.

But Will grinned up at her and heaved Nero over a spot, patting the space beside him. "Hike your skirts and sit a spell, got a great story for all of you."

He crossed his legs in front of him, bony knees sticking out of burn holes in his pants and launched right into his tale, waving his arms, all excited.

Will began his story right where he had last seen the two boys. "When I left you guys at the depot, I ran home. I could see fire that way, even though it's about two miles from town," he said, still waving his arms. "I reached Anderson's farm and found Andy, but his big dog stopped us from going any farther. Good thing too. We never would have made it. Fire swooped down on us in a flash and a roar. Trees, houses, barn, haystacks, everything at once. Andy and I staggered through burning brush and terrible thick smoke. We reached a river and jumped in. Ducked under and hunkered down." Will swiveled his arms and pointed like he was showing them through the woods.

"Never thought we'd make it out alive, but we did," Will said, shaking his head. He grinned at them. "And when we climbed out that night, guess what? My two brothers came walking by. They had gotten as far as Nortenson's and had gone in the river just a ways downstream from us."

Will got up on his knees, needing more room to gesture. "We'd just settled down for the night in a little blacksmith shop that hadn't burned when along came my Pa. My whole family had been saved in the river. The same river. They had gone in about a mile farther downstream." Will grew quiet, looking curiously at Tony.

Tears ran down Tony's cheeks, but he smiled slightly at Will. Maggie reached over and took Tony's hand.

"I'm sure glad for you," said Tony. "How'd you get back here?"

"Walked back this morning with Jack McGowan," said Will. He sat back down and held up his feet. "See my new rubbers? I'd lost my shoes in the river. Found these at the hermit's shack, you know him? The fellow who makes them for the lumberjacks? Everything at the McGowan's was burned except their cookstove." A dimple deepened in Will's cheek as he grinned. "We looked it over to see if it was still workable. I opened the oven door, and there was a live chicken in there! It must have jumped in when the door was open and then the wind blew the door shut. I wouldn't let the others kill it to eat. I'm going to keep it as a pet."

Will's story was like a breath of fresh air. They all laughed with him, even Tony. Nero barked joyfully, wagging his tail and giving everyone sloppy kisses. It was all so unreal to Maggie that she put a hand over her mouth to stop laughing, afraid she would turn hysterical. The workers unloading the boxes of relief supplies gave them a strange look. Maggie was sure they thought those poor kids had lost their minds. Dr. Stephan came over and put his hand on Tony's shoulder.

"I'm going to send you to Pine City to have that burn on your chest tended to," he said. "I'll let Clara and your aunt and uncle know you're there. They'll be down as soon as they can."

Tony looked up at Dr. Stephan with sad, sad eyes. "Before I go, can I show you where my parents are, and my brother? So you can take care of things? Can Pastor Knudsen sort of have a funeral or something?"

Tears streamed down Maggie's face. How could they have been laughing just a moment before? Tony planning a funeral all by himself! The worst thing in the world to do, and he was doing it all alone. She sidled up next to him, put her arm around him.

"We'll help too," she said, gently but firmly. "We'll all help."

Pastor and Mrs. Knudsen were right there.

"Of course, lad," said the pastor.

Mrs. Knudsen put her arms around Tony. "I'll be with you every moment until your sister and relatives get here."

Everyone started to get teary, till Nero jumped up on Mrs. Knudsen to crowd himself into her hug with a woofy wet kiss.

Later they all met at the relief train to see Tony off to Pine City. The boys slapped backs and punched shoulders. "We'll always be buddies," said Will.

"Always stay together," added Jack.

They spit in their palms and stacked their fists together.

"Get back here as soon as you can," said Jack. "We'll be staying in tents. Maybe the three of us can have our own tent." He hugged the slobbery, grinning dog. "All four of us," he corrected.

Maggie hugged Tony good-bye, and he gave her a shy, grateful smile. As the train pulled away, Maggie watched Jack and Will run off together, tripping over Nero, back to the food line. How close those boys were. Eddie and Tom had been too.

Maggie hadn't made a friend like that in Hinckley, not close giggly girlfriends like Nancy and Suzy had been in Superior. But then, she had never tried. If she'd made more of an effort, she and Mary and Clara would have been close too. Maybe they still could be. But the town was destroyed. Hinckley was gone forever. She'd missed her chance.

Maggie turned back to help Gramma. Standing in a stack of boxes shoulder-height, Gramma was digging through and unpacking pots and pans, sorting them by size and purpose. She clutched a big enamel coffeepot that she wouldn't set down.

Maggie noticed a large stack of lumber had also been unloaded. Puzzled, she asked Papa, "What's that for? What are they going to build?"

Papa's large hands rubbed his forehead.

"Coffins," he said softly.

INTERMENT
September 2 and 3, 1894

Clang! Clang! Clang! Maggie banged her ladle against a triangle-shaped dinner gong, calling anyone within hearing distance to a noon meal. Nero, lying tied to a tent stake with a length of hayrope, sat up and she absentmindedly patted his head. He lay down again, his big head resting on outstretched paws. Securing the flap of the large mess tent, she looked out over the wretched landscape.

Two orderly rows of white canvas army tents, already darkened by smoke and soot, lined up in military formation to house relief crews. Beyond lay the smoking and smoldering ruins of the village of Hinckley. Yet farther beyond stretched acres of scorched black earth, skeletons of tree trunks, gaping holes in the ground that once supported foundations of buildings. Volunteer workers gathered the dead into buggies, buckboards, and hay wagons. No battlefield could have looked worse.

Survivors and relief workers, backs bent and heads bowed, straggled to the tent. Horror and shock had been etched deeply into their faces. None raised eyes to Maggie. Silently they walked through the food line and found places at the long trestle tables.

"Those men look like death warmed over," Maggie told Gramma. But it heartened her to see Gramma looking better. Last night in their tent, they had scrubbed themselves and their clothes, washed their hair, and slept in clean cots on warm woolen army blankets. Gramma had fussed a bit about not having good lye soap and bleach for their aprons. Good sign, thought Maggie.

Gramma watched the men file in. "It's like hope has died," she said. "They've lost their friends and loved ones. Just being here is devastating."

Gloom wrapped its cold arms around Maggie, and she shivered.

"When we lost your mother," Gramma mused, "neighbors brought food. They all told us they would miss her and sat and had coffee with us. A gentle word, a touch, a cup of coffee."

Maggie doubted that would help, but she took one coffeepot and Gramma took the other to the men seated at long rows of wooden planks set on sawhorses. Maggie put her hand on each shoulder.

"More coffee?" she asked, refilling their cups.

The men, soot-blackened faces etched with grief, turned and looked up at her.

"Thanks, miss," they murmured. Soon they began talking to each other. Sad voices, but at least, voices.

Back at the cookstove refilling pots, Maggie burst out, "Gramma, nothing can get better until we all leave. How much longer will we have to stay here? It's so dreadful."

"I know it's dreadful, dear," Gramma said. "But the need is so great. How could we leave now?"

A deep sigh welled up inside Maggie. Gramma was right. Her family had been so fortunate. How could they refuse to help others, no matter how hard it was to do?

Finished with serving, Gramma and Maggie filled tin cups for themselves and sat on the long plank bench by Papa, Eddie, and Jack. Across the table sat Dr. Cowan and Dr. Stephan, Pastor Knudsen, Angus Hay, and Frank Webber, a mortician from Pine City. Dr. Cowan, elbows on the table, held a steaming tin cup in his hands.

"I guess I'm the official coroner," he said. "Dr. Stephan and I will need to keep records of all we bury. Name, age, where found, how identified." He frowned down the table at the others. "A great many will never be identified. . . ."

Angus Hay added, "I'll keep similar records for insurance purposes. Survivors will need documents to make claims." He pulled his gaze away from the desolate sight beyond the tent door and looked at Papa. "Jules, Mayor Webster's wife is missing, and he's in no shape to direct burial activities. I expect there'll be hundreds of bodies, way too many for us to dig individual graves. Not enough time and not enough space. We'll have to bury them together in mass graves. Will you see about digging trenches?"

Papa nodded wordlessly, his hand rubbing his forehead.

Mr. Webber stood and put on his black bowler hat. "Everyone who has come with wagons, hayracks, or buggies is directed to find and bring bodies to the cemetery east of town. Starting with the town streets." He left quickly.

Maggie, sad-eyed and bereft, sat as the others quietly followed. Her stomach ached again.

"Come now," said Gramma, gathering plates and cups. "We need to keep meals ready for whenever anyone comes in."

A long, low, mournful train whistle sounded down the track, and Maggie watched from the tent door as another relief train pulled in. She wondered if all these people who came to help realized what they were getting themselves into. How death and decay and overwhelming grief would grasp them, engulf them with sights and smells that would haunt them the rest of their lives.

A small, serious gentleman disembarked and surveyed the scene. Mr. Webber greeted him. The gentleman pointed toward an open boxcar. High stacks of wooden boxes. More coffins.

"I'm a mortician from St. Paul," said the newcomer. "I brought these with me. Twenty-three of them," his face twitched, "but they're all filled with bodies we found alongside the tracks between here and Pine City."

Maggie quickly darted back inside the tent.

She and Gramma kept busy feeding burial crews that afternoon. Several times Maggie watched through misty eyes as wagons went back and forth endlessly between the streets of the town and the cemetery. A great many more wagons brought bodies in from the surrounding countryside—from every farm, from every lumbercamp. And what had happened to Wacouta and the Chippewa hunting camp?

Eddie and Jack returned in the early evening. Gramma sat them at a table, intent on getting food into them. Jack had untied Nero, who followed the boy into the tent and lay at his feet. Maggie sat too, not hungry but needing their company. The boys seemed not to notice the plates Gramma set before them, not touching knife or fork.

"Been digging long trenches all day," said Eddie, staring blindly across the table. "Thirty-three bodies were brought back from Skunk Lake and along that track. Wrapped in blankets, thank God."

"Ninety-six bodies were brought in from the swamp north of the Grindstone River," said Jack, his voice husky. "Where Tony lost his family. Pastor Knudsen buried Tony's family this morning. I . . . I represented our family at the graveside. I thought Tony would like that." He sniffed a little, blew his nose into a dirty handkerchief. "Most of the others were put in the trench. No one could tell who they were." Nero sat up and nosed Jack's hand. Jack leaned over and hugged the big dog, burying his face in deep fur.

Maggie didn't like this. Jack should not be out there. He should be . . . be where? She looked at Gramma. Shouldn't Gramma keep him here in camp?

Gramma shrugged her shoulders. Jack wouldn't stay in camp, Maggie realized. Even if told to stay, he would go out with the men to help. Not good, though—he'd likely have nightmares the rest of his life. Gramma poured coffee, adding sugar and milk.

"Eat now," she insisted. "Hot food will keep body and soul together."

The boys began eating, then cleaned their plates, not realizing how hungry they had been.

"Papa told us to get some rest," Eddie said, "but he's going to keep working by lantern light. Dr. Cowan says the bodies should be buried as soon as possible." He got up and walked toward an adjacent tent where cots were set up.

"Wake me at first light," he said, his voice very tired, very sad. Jack, already half-asleep, followed by Nero, went with Eddie.

Maggie watched them go. At least, Jack could always sleep. Papa ought to sleep too. She looked out again toward the cemetery beyond the edge of town, beyond the destroyed homes and businesses. Light faded, slowly retreated, deserting the day. The landscape was bare, black, and wretched, broken only by jagged burned tree stumps. Bent, silhouetted men dug with ax and shovel.

She needed to see Papa, to talk with him. Badly enough to walk over there. He would need to see her too. Gramma, uneasy about Maggie going to the cemetery, reluctantly packaged up a lunch to take to Papa and gave her a coffeepot. Maggie swallowed hard and began the trek.

Even near dusk, the day was still hot. There was a terrible smell in the air, and Maggie realized with a jolt why the burials needed to be done quickly. She nearly turned around and went back. She stopped and took deep breaths. She thought of Mama.

Of Mama standing beside her, brushing her hair back from her face, like she always did when Maggie was fretful. Calmness settled around her like a soft blanket.

Mama wasn't dead and gone forever and forgotten by everyone and never talked about. Everyone remembered Mama, thought about what she had done, what she would do if she were still alive. And all of these people being buried here would be remembered and loved and thought about. Loving didn't stop. A tear traced unnoticed down Maggie's cheek. She walked on toward Papa.

Nearing the graveyard, Maggie heard shovels scraping, pickaxes clanking. She saw two long dirt mounds, heaped over with scorched black earth. Men were digging two more trenches. Bewildered survivors, clearly in shock, searched for missing loved ones among the rows of bodies. Some people who had identified family members were digging separate graves for them. Maggie's heart ached with pity. All too well, she remembered Mama's burial. It had been so hard. So hard for so long.

Papa found her standing there and held her awhile. "As if things weren't bad enough, it brings Mama's funeral all back, doesn't it?" he asked gently.

A trembling sigh escaped Maggie. "I was thinking of that too," she said. "But how terrible to have lost whole families. How can they stand it?"

Papa tightened his arm around her. "You go on because others need you," he said. "And your friends and loved ones hold you up, and you keep going for their sake. And because Mama would want us to."

Maggie didn't say anything. Mama would want them to go on, to help each other.

Mama would be doing everything she could to help here.

Papa led her to a scorched but still intact log, and they sat down. Maggie reached into her package of food and pulled out bread and boiled beef.

"Here, Papa. Gramma says you should eat."

Papa ate only one bite of the sandwich but accepted the cup of coffee she poured. Maggie felt better, glad to be with Papa. It almost felt as if Mama were with them.

They watched the burials. At one end of the long, deep trench, men stood on the brink leaning on shovels. As a farm wagon pulled up at the far end, four men reached into it, bringing out long poles and blankets.

"What are those for?" Maggie whispered to Papa.

"They make stretchers to carry the bodies," he answered. The tailgate of the wagon lowered, and two men put victims on the stretchers, carrying them to the edge of the trench, down an incline about four feet deep. Gently the bodies, wrapped in blankets, were laid next to each other, row on row on row, in the long ditch. The wooden coffins and lumber had all been used up. Maggie had to hold her apron closely over her nose and mouth.

Mr. Webber joined them. Maggie quickly poured him a cup of coffee. He pulled down a handkerchief he had stretched over his nose and mouth and took long grateful swallows, then motioned toward a wagon being unloaded.

"Eighteen bodies found in an old well," he said. "The fire sucked out all the oxygen, and they suffocated. Mercifully. Another group over there," he indicated, "found an entire family in their cellar, also suffocated." He lit a cigar, breathing in the much more pleasant odor of tobacco smoke.

Papa accepted a cigar Mr. Webber offered him.

"Hinckley's dead are nearly all gathered," he said, striking a match on his boot sole.

"Lots of folks still searching the countryside yet," said Mr. Webber.

"How much longer will it all take?" Maggie asked.

Papa breathed out a long wavering ribbon of cigar smoke and said, "By tomorrow night, we should have our area fairly well cleared. Sandstone, Brook Park, all the other towns have crews working. But I have the feeling we'll be finding victims for a long time."

Across the long mound, two young brothers dug a separate family grave several yards away. Seven boxes were stacked beside the dark hole.

Pastor Knudsen came up beside them, and they all sat on the log. He took her hand.

"How are you doing?" he asked. "Should you be out here?"

"I feel better when I'm by Papa," Maggie said.

Pastor Knudsen smiled at her. "We're all better for your being here," he said. He brushed wispy bangs off her forehead. "You and Alma are like angels among us. Bless you for being here."

"Just like her mama would have been," Papa added. Somewhat embarrassed, Maggie straightened her apron and refilled everyone's cups, whether they were empty or not.

"We'll have a burial service tomorrow evening," said Pastor. "All the local clergy will participate. These deaths were so grievous, they should be laid to rest with respect and dignity, their souls committed to heaven."

The long black mounds stretched in front of Maggie. She struggled to keep her composure in front of the men.

"I wish we had flowers," she whispered.

PLANS & DECISIONS
September 8, 1894

Maggie hurried to the plank trestle table where Papa,
Eddie, and Jack finished breakfast, Jack not-so-secretly
slipping scraps down under the table to Nero.
Gramma, carrying her ever-steaming pot of coffee, followed Maggie. Papa had delayed leaving when the
workmen and the volunteers had left, and the family
had the tent to themselves. The morning breeze gently
flapped the canvas tent wall. The air finally was beginning to smell fresh again.

Papa smiled around the table.

"Thank the Good Lord we were all spared. We've
gone through a tragic week, but the dead are laid to rest,
and we can begin the rest of our lives."

Maggie's throat tightened. The rest of their lives
would never be the same. Gramma dabbed at her eyes,
then rubbed her spectacles with her handkerchief.

"So now," Papa continued, "what lies ahead? The
railroads are back on schedule. Eddie and I are back at

work, and for us nothing has changed. We need to stay in Hinckley. I've applied to the Relief Commission to have our house rebuilt. Until it's done, Eddie and I will live in an army tent."

Maggie's heart thudded. Surely Papa wouldn't keep them here now? Home could never be here in Hinckley! Hinckley would forever be a place of tragedy, of death, and of destruction. She looked at Gramma. Gramma was still dabbing her eyes.

Jack jumped up. "I'm going to stay with you," he insisted. "School starts soon, maybe in a tent at first, but Will says the brick schoolhouse will be rebuilt just like the old one. We can help rebuild it, Will says." Jack's eyes shone. He could hardly stand still. "I can help build our house too. Can I have my own room?"

Maggie's mouth dropped open. Jack wanted to stay here? After all he'd been through? She stared at him. Jack grinned at her like he expected her to be excited too. Like he thought rebuilding Hinckley would be the greatest adventure of their lives.

Before Papa could speak, Gramma put on her spectacles and cleared her throat.

"You can't stay here by yourselves. Who would look after you? Cook, clean, wash clothes? Get you off to school and work? I will stay too." She gave Papa a stern no-nonsense look over the top of her gold rims. "Jules, you see to that relief house immediately. I've heard that includes furnishings too. And I want two lots, so we can have a chicken yard and a buggy shed." She nodded decisively, her mind set. Stunned, Maggie couldn't speak. Rebuild a town, a home on ashes surrounded by graves? Live where grief ruled every thought? Where every step they took immersed them in remembered tragedy? They would relive that horror every day!

Papa put his large hand over Maggie's trembling one. "Don't look so stricken, Missy. Pastor Knudsen found a board-and-room position for you with Reverend Ecklund in Superior. You can live with the Ecklunds in the parsonage in exchange for helping Mrs. Ecklund with housekeeping." He smiled gently at her. "It's all arranged. You can move in next Sunday and start classes at your old school the next day."

Maggie tried to look at Papa's face, but it was all blurry because her eyes were streaming tears. Papa had found a place for her to live in Superior. Papa understood how she needed the comfort of a safe home— away from Hinckley's ghosts and from a life that would be haunted by terrible memories. Now she could go back to her own school, with Suzy and Nancy. She'd live in a proper house, surrounded by tall green trees and the great sparkling lake.

"Thank you, thank you, Papa." She jumped up and

hugged him, wiping away tears.

He held her tightly, not saying anything. No one said anything. The boys sat quietly, heads down. Gramma was dabbing again.

Slowly Maggie sank back into her chair, looking from one sad face to the other. If she left, the family wouldn't be together anymore. Knots started to tangle her stomach as she looked at Jack, bent over Nero, face in his fur. Eddie whittled on a chunk of pinewood, giving it lots of attention. As glad as she would be to leave Hinckley, she wondered if she could leave her brothers, her family. After having had to face the fact that she may have lost her brothers, then, thank God, finally finding them, could she really leave them again? Finding them, being together, was such a blessing.

But, she reasoned, she wouldn't be leaving them, exactly. She'd only be gone during the week for school. She'd come home weekends and could help with the house and be with the family, then escape back to the peace and beauty of Superior. That would work. She looked at Papa with a bright smile.

"I can come back on weekends, can't I, Papa? It will be just like going away to boarding school." That would work just fine.

"Something like that," said Papa, nodding slowly, "depending on railroad schedules and Pastor Ecklund's schedule. His wife may need you to clean on some weekends." He pulled out his pipe and tobacco pouch. "It'll all work itself out."

Maggie's thoughts raced ahead to what her room at the Ecklund's would be like. Would she have a view of the lake? Clothes! She looked at her torn, singed dress. She had nothing to wear.

"Gramma, what . . . ?"

Gramma knew what she meant.

"There's a relief train due today with clothes and linens and such, from the Ladies Relief in Duluth. You'll look proper and citified in no time." She rummaged through her pockets for a dry handkerchief.

Maggie gazed out the open tent flap. A breeze stirred up the ashes covering the bare ground. Soon she'd have a window to look out of, with a tall tree alongside. Maybe a view of Lake Superior. And she'd be able to forget the horror of Hinckley, bury all the terrible memories in a big mass grave in the back of her mind.

* * * *

"Maggie! Maggie!" a girl's voice yelled outside the tent. "Maggie!" The voice sounded closer, like someone running. Maggie dashed to the tent flap and looked out.

"Mary! Clara!" called Maggie. "You're back. When did you get here? Did you come to help with the clean-up?" She dashed out and hugged both girls. All three crying, they stepped back and smiled and hugged again. Maggie's heart bubbled with joy at seeing them, and she quickly wiped tears away. She was surprised at how glad she was to know that they were safe and sound. To know how much she cared for them.

Gramma and Papa came out to join the hug. Eddie and Jake followed with big grins, obviously not knowing if they should hug the girls or shake hands or what. Papa motioned the boys over with his head, and Maggie scooped them into the same hug. Nero raced around them, poking his head into gaps between bodies till everyone stepped back, and Jack petted the dog quiet.

"Are you here to stay?" Papa asked Clara. "Will you and Tony stay here with Mary's family? One big family?"

Jack perked up. "Tony? Is he here with you?"

"He'll be here in a day or so," said Clara, her hand holding tightly to Gramma's arm around her waist. Gramma gave her one of her "love you," grandmotherly smiles. "Mary and I came in on the relief train."

"My papa and mama are here too," said Mary. "Papa's seeing to building us a new house. A big one." She smiled a sisterly smile at Clara, squeezing her other hand.

Maggie looked beyond their close group. A relief train stood by the former depot site. The area had been cleared of all burned debris—another military tent now served the railroad's needs. Lots of unloading going on over there. Lots of big boxes.

"There's tons of relief supplies," said Mary. "We're going to unpack clothes and household supplies and stuff for the folks who will rebuild. Sort of a big "free" store."

"Lots of nice clothes for ladies," said Clara, smiling. "We peeked."

"Can you help us?" Mary asked Maggie. "We'll get first pick of things. Not too many folks back here yet, but they'll be coming. Those survivors still in Duluth are getting restless." She turned all around, surveying the former town. There were still lots of wagons moving through streets, now carrying away charred metal remains of the fire—stoves, pots and pans, iron bedsteads and coil springs. Some folks were raking ashes off their lot as if they were raking fall leaves off the lawn. "I see the debris is nearly all cleared away. Building can start soon."

Gramma squeezed the girls in another brief hug.

"Go see to the clothes," she said. "I'll have to stay working here in the mess tent, but tell everyone to come back for cookies and coffee whenever they can take a moment away. I want to hear all the news."

"Cookies, Gramma Grant?" asked Clara. "Where will you get cookies?"

Gramma's eyes twinkled. "These big army stoves have room for everything a body could want. Ovens big enough for three turkeys. Might be, I'll keep this one. Trade it for my services, or some such."

Laughing, the girls trotted back to the train, holding hands and swinging their arms. All three wearing their hair in long braids.

"If you see anything that would fit me, set it aside," Gramma called after them. "I'll be able to come down after dinner to 'shop.'"

"I can't wait for school to start," said Mary. "I think we'll be the only girls in the upper class. We'll be able to boss all the littler kids."

"We'll get all the chores, more likely," said Clara. "All the cleaning, recess duties, slapping erasers, and washing slate boards." Her voice was soft and serious, but Maggie saw a teasing smile tweak the corners of her mouth. She realized Clara was thinking more about returning to an orderly life than just to school.

"Won't take long between the three of us," said Mary. "We'll still have plenty of time to flirt with the boys." To demonstrate, she fluttered her long blond eyelashes.

Maggie swallowed around a lump in her throat. "I won't be going to school here," she said. "I'll be going to my old school in Superior. Boarding with a preacher Pastor Knudsen knows." She struggled to keep a smile on her face.

Mary and Clara stopped in the road, a slight breeze billowing gray ashes across the bare ground. They looked at each other, then at Maggie. Mary nibbled the edge of her fingernail, and Clara brushed at the corner of her eye, pretending dust had blown in it.

"But my family is rebuilding our house. I'll be back weekends." Maggie tilted her head, looking quizzically at the girls. "Do you really want to live here? It's like living in a graveyard." As soon as the words were spoken, Maggie clapped her hands over her mouth. "Oh, Clara, I'm so sorry."

Clara took both Maggie's hands in hers. "Don't be sorry, Maggie. Of course I've had those same thoughts. I had to work through all that before I could even come here. So has everyone who went through this."

"I'm so sorry you lost your family," said Maggie. Tears coursed down her face. "I'll never forget what it was like when I lost my mother. It's all so hard. Are you sure this is where you want to be? Don't you just want to go away and leave it all behind?"

Clara cried in her arms. "You were so good to Tony after the fire. You and Jack were there for him when no one else was around, and it helped him so much because of what you two said about your mother and all." She stood back and wiped her eyes with a hanky Mary handed her. "But leaving Hinckley would be like leaving my family all behind. I feel better being here. Like I'm still near them."

Maggie's mouth dropped open. That's exactly how she had felt about leaving Superior! She wiped away her own tears. But all her memories of her mother were placed in Superior. Happy memories there, terrible memories here.

"I understand why you need to be here," Maggie said slowly. "But won't you also constantly be reminded of tragedy here? How can you be happy here?"

"I probably won't be really happy for a long time yet," said Clara. "But I'll be with family and friends, and I'll be busy doing useful work. Time will heal it all. That's what everyone tells me." She paused and looked thoughtfully at Maggie. "Was that true for you?"

Maggie blinked, and a last tear trickled down her cheek. She had never given that much thought.

"I guess it is," she said. "It's nice to remember Mama now. I'll never stop missing her, but I can remember the good times without feeling quite so much grief. It doesn't hurt my heart like it used to."

Clara sighed. "You've already helped Tony, and now you've helped me. A tiny bit, but tiny bits add up."

The girls turned and walked on down to the relief tent. It was time to think of finding clean clothes and soap and towels. And aprons for Gramma.

A ROOM WITH A VIEW
December 13, 1894

Maggie's eyes snapped open, she flew up with a start that nearly threw her out of bed. Heart thumping, whamming against her chest like it would bust through, she gasped for a breath, staring frantically into total consuming darkness. Dread filled her, surrounded her, silenced her scream, paralyzed everything but her pounding heart. Where was Jack? Where was Eddie?

The dream again. The terrifying dream.

She dropped her head in her hands, willing her heart to slow down, breathing deeply. Oddly, the flaming visions in the recurring nightmare faded quickly, always leaving Maggie with an overwhelming feeling of hopeless dread. She fell back and burrowed under her quilt, clutching Mama's pillow, knowing she wouldn't fall back asleep.

Where would Jack be these days? Probably ice-fishing. He loved the lakes, winter and summer. But, she worried, he never gave a thought to how thin the ice was, how bitter the wind, how quickly snow flurries could whip up, sur-round and disorient a person. And Eddie? No matter how wintry the night, he'd be out chopping and stacking wood for Gramma. Heading off south till he found timber, then hauling it back home. Got back pretty late some nights but always went out again the next night. Work till he'd be so tired and numb from cold, he'd be near to chopping his own foot off.

Or maybe the two of them would be out hunting, rang-ing farther and farther from home, probably getting them-selves lost in a blizzard. How could she ever find them in a blizzard? She understood Gramma a lot better now. Needing to be with someone to care for them, like you were the only one who could keep them safe.

Maggie stared at the dark glass rectangle on the wall that allowed in a bit of dim starlight, waiting to hear Pastor rattle the coal stove downstairs, her signal to get up and get through another day.

Racing up the icy schoolhouse steps, Maggie slipped in the door just as the warning bell rang. She unwrapped herself, tossing coat, hat, scarf, and mittens in the direction of a coat hook and raced into her homeroom, dropping breathless into her desk as the final bell shrilled through the now-empty hallway.

Giggles rippled from the seat behind her, and a pen-cil poked her shoulder.

"Pastor and Mrs. Ecklund want a big breakfast this morning?" Nancy's voice whispered.

"Pastor's list of chores must be as long as his sermons," added Suzy, snickering.

Maggie turned in her seat, showing them her reddened rough hands. "Look, dishpan hands," she whispered, not altogether faking her dismay. "I'd show you my housemaid's knees if I weren't wearing long johns."

Teacher's ruler rapped sharply on his desk. Maggie welcomed immersing her mind in the orderly studies. She knew, deep down, that she liked school not so much because it was in Superior and she was with old friends, but because it controlled time, kept her mind busy. She seemed to need controlled, predictable blocks of time. Panic never caught her in school.

* * * *

Sitting across the lunchroom table from Nancy and Suzy, Maggie opened her lunchpail. She unfolded a sheet of brown paper and set out her lunch: a fried slab of cornmeal mush, a small glass jar of applesauce, and a rind of fried pork. Leftovers from the Ecklunds' breakfast. She glanced across at Nancy's white cloth napkin, on which sat a sandwich of white bread and sliced turkey and pickles. Suzy had a cold fried chicken leg and a covered bowl of groundcherry sauce.

Suzy lifted an eyebrow as she looked at Maggie's

pork rind. "Do the Ecklunds eat that stuff? Bet they have goose grease on rye bread for supper too."

Maggie picked it up and turned it in her hand. "Oh, well," she said. "I'm not so fussy anymore. Food was hard to come by after the fire. We were glad to get anything that would hold body and soul together."

Laughing, Nancy said, "Clothes must have been hard to come by too. Haven't you got anything that wasn't from Relief?" She put her sandwich down and looked at Maggie's frayed shirtwaist. "Are you coming to the Christmas dance Friday night? What will you wear?" She peered under the table. "You can't dance in those shoes."

"You haven't come Christmas caroling with us, or come to any taffy pulls, or gone sledding or skating. Nothing," Suzy observed. "Work, work, work. Don't you want to have some fun? Stay here next weekend. Shop for some new clothes."

"It's the one weekend a month I can go to Hinckley," Maggie protested. "I'm not going to miss Christmas with my family. There'll be lots to do—Gramma will need help. The relief house isn't quite finished. Woodwork needs varnishing, rag rugs still need to be braided. We have to find china plates somewhere, and foods for Christmas dinner, like herring and honey and cinnamon sticks and ginger. And cookie cutters, for goodness sakes. Where can I get tin cookie cutters?"

Nancy and Suzy exchanged "told-you-so" looks.

"Emily's over there," said Nancy, looking away. "Let's ask her to stay over with us after the party."

Leaving the remnants of their lunches on the table, Nancy and Suzy jumped up and left Maggie sitting.

"At least Emily'll talk about something besides that everlasting fire recovery," said Suzy, not making any effort to speak softly. "Who cares about varnish and cookie cutters anyway?"

* * * *

Late afternoon sunlight sparkled on the fresh-fallen snow, giving it a golden glint as Maggie and Papa walked to the Superior Depot after his regular Sunday afternoon visit. Their boots made little squeaky noises as they scrunched over the packed snow. Papa had an hour's time between arrivals and departures.

"You'll ride home with me on Christmas Eve," said Papa, "and come back to Superior on Christmas Day on my evening run." He squeezed her mittened hand with his big, gloved one. "Gramma has plans to invite a goose for dinner."

"I can hardly wait, Papa," said Maggie. "I wish I could stay longer."

"It can't be helped," said Papa, forced cheerfulness in his voice. "Christmas is a busy season for Pastor

Ecklund." He quickened his pace. "Time's a-flying, Missy. I have to be on duty in half an hour." Talking quickly, he related the news from home.

"We're nearly settled in the new house. Would be, but Gramma keeps the boys rearranging the furniture every few days. She's anxious for your suggestions." His voice rose an excited notch. "There's one hundred and fifty homes finished now, another one hundred under construction. Sixty students in the school! There's a hotel and a barbershop and a blacksmith shop and a general store ... " Papa ran on and on again, this time making Maggie smile.

"Jack wants to keep a stray cat that "followed" him home," Papa chuckled. "He's trying to convince Gramma it's his civic duty to provide for the homeless."

Maggie wondered how Nero would react to a cat. Probably lick it to death. Suddenly she missed Nero and his big slobbery kisses.

All too soon they reached the depot. Giving Maggie a hug and a kiss and saying "see you in a week, Missy," Papa hurried into the station. Maggie set off for home at a brisk pace. The sun set early in winter, and the temperature dropped quickly.

She let herself in the front door of the gray stone parsonage, its interior dark, chilly, and quiet. The Ecklunds were at evening services. Maggie hung her coat on the hall coatrack and climbed the stairs. The second floor had three bedrooms, but Mrs. Ecklund had situated Maggie in the former maid's quarters in the attic.

Maggie entered her room, the slight squeak of the door sounding very loud. Her room contained a single iron bed, a commode, and a small desk and chair. She took a candle stub from the desk drawer. There was a kerosene lantern, but Pastor Ecklund only allowed her to use it for studying. Kerosene was dear, he explained. A candle was sufficient when she wasn't doing schoolwork.

Hanging her Sunday dress on its hook, Maggie climbed into her nightclothes. Thank goodness Gramma had found her a flannel nightgown! A soft, warm, pretty nightgown that someone had given the relief organizations out of love and kindness. Love and kindness that warmed body and soul. The only heat came through a grate in the floor, all the way up from the parlor. Not that Pastor kept the parlor stove stoked all the time. Coal must be dear too.

Maggie wrapped a quilt around her shoulders, cradled her now-ragged pillow in her arm, and sat on the window seat in the dormer. Leaning her head against the wall, she stared out the frosted glass at the frozen distant lake. The scratching of icy, bare branches against the windowpane echoed through the big empty house.

BEING ALONE IS WORSE
December 25, 1894

Clink, clank, clatter. Rattling pots, pans, and dishes woke Maggie. She stretched and blinked as bright sunshine reflected off the whitewashed ceiling into her eyes. Where was she? Someplace warm and soft and not very quiet. Ah, yes. Home with Papa and Gramma and the boys. In Gramma's downy featherbed, on Christmas Day. A sudden, pleased smile spread across her face. She'd slept well and deep—no dreams.

And she'd not have to get up in the dark and cold this morning to stoke the stoves, to make the Ecklunds' breakfast, and trudge off to school. Snuggling deeper under the quilts, she pulled the pillows around her to make a nest. A big calico cat settled itself in the curve of Maggie's knees. She could hear Gramma downstairs, hers and Papa's voices, happy and laughing, not making much effort to be quiet. Maggie had to smile at Gramma's way of getting people up—laugh them awake.

It never worked too well with Jack, she remembered.

Anxiety suddenly gripped her, and Maggie had to get up, to check on them, to make sure they were here and well. She slipped out of bed, crossed the cold floor, hustled through the hallway, and peeked in the doorway of Jack and Eddie's bedroom. A heap of quilts on both beds stirred, then settled down again with soft snores. Maggie smiled to herself. God bless them, she thought. She went back to bed and snuggled under the quilt.

But Papa's booming laugh and Gramma's quiet chuckle echoed up the stairs. An aroma of fresh hot coffee swirled its way up to the bedroom, drifting in as surely as if it were invited. So who could sleep late on Christmas morning? Maggie threw off the covers, dressed quickly, and scurried down the narrow stairway to the kitchen. The cat, after a long stretch and yawn, followed her down. Gramma was busy stuffing a goose. Papa looked up from his newspaper, a steaming coffee cup in one hand.

"Merry Christmas, Missy," he said, a big grin on his face, pulling out the chair next to him. Gramma glanced up, eyes merry over her spectacles.

"Merry Christmas, Papa and Gramma," said Maggie. She gave them each a quick kiss, helped herself to a warm slice of coffeecake, and took a big bite of the soft cinnamon bread. Melted butter trickled down her fingers, chased by a tiny avalanche of streusel.

Gramma tucked the goose into the roaster and put it in the oven. She had indeed acquired a big handsome cookstove, complete with gleaming chrome handles. Patting her hands on her apron, she sat down and refilled the coffee cups.

"Land sakes," she said, "last September, who would have thought that we would have such a wonderful Christmas?" A little burbling noise from the back of the stove called Gramma, and she popped back up to add more milk to a pot of rice.

Maggie tipped a little white pitcher and poured cream into her coffee. Real cream, she noticed. Gramma and Jack must be trading again.

"We're luckier than most folks," Papa mused, the laughter fading from his voice. "Most families in Hinckley have empty places around their tables."

Maggie had been amazed at all the new houses in Hinckley. Lots of people had rebuilt, even after family members were dead and buried. Often she thought about what Clara had said—that staying here was a comfort. Maggie could understand how that was true for Clara and probably for anyone else whose family had roots here. And happy memories. . . .

"I understand Pastor Knudsen and Father Lawler have made sure no one is alone today," said Gramma, punctuating her remark with a wooden spoon. "Thank the Good Lord, we're all together."

Thunder reverberated down the stairway, and Jack and Eddie burst into the kitchen.

"Merry Christmas," yelled Jack. "Let's open presents!"

Gramma wagged her dripping spoon at him. "Breakfast first, then church."

Jack stopped still, eyeing Gramma with his pleading puppy-dog eyes. Maggie laughed, figuring he had perfected his technique by observing Nero. She glanced around, wondering where the big dog was. A loud woof from the back porch and wet noseprints on the window answered that question. Gramma must have drawn the line at allowing Nero indoors now that the house was finished.

"Fresh hot streusel coffeecake?" Gramma suggested.

Easily persuaded, Jack slipped into the chair beside Maggie and grinned at her. "I see you came home with lots of bundles. For under the tree?" he asked.

She ruffled his hair. "Right after church."

Laughing, Eddie winked at her across the table as he buttered his coffeecake.

* * * *

Church services were held in the temporary schoolhouse. Pastor Knudsen greeted everyone at the door with a handshake. "Good to see you home, Maggie," he said and inquired after the Ecklunds.

"Just fine," Maggie said, wondering if they had managed to make their own breakfast. Settling onto a wood plank pew, her gaze wandered the one-room schoolhouse. Pine boughs draped gracefully from the ceiling, fastened at the corners with red ribbons. Where had anyone found live pine boughs, wondered Maggie.

Jack poked her in the ribs.

"Look up front by the desk. On the floor," he whispered, loudly enough so he needn't have whispered. Boxes wrapped with bits of ribbon and lace were stacked beside a pile of brown paper bags, tops twisted shut. "Presents, do you suppose?"

"Shush," Gramma whispered. "You're in church." A suppressed smile burst through her frown. "You'll have something to take home."

Services began with a rousing chorus of "Joy to the World," rattling the rafters of the drafty wood building. Pastor Knudsen pointed out that the Christ Child had been born in even humbler circumstances but was surrounded by the love of family and friends and angels. His sermon was unusually short, and Maggie gave Gramma a questioning look when Pastor finished abruptly.

"Presbyterians worship at eight A.M., the Lutherans at nine, and the Catholics at ten," Gramma said. "We all use the schoolhouse, which makes for short services." A tiny chuckle escaped her. "Being in the middle, we get a chance to visit with everyone coming and going. The Presbyterians are planning a pie sale to raise money for their new church." Maggie could see Gramma loved the sharing arrangement.

After the last amen, Mary and Clara ran up to them.

"Maggie!" they said, both hugging her at once. "How long can you stay? Can you come over to our house?"

"Oh, I can't," Maggie said, her smile drooping. "I have to go back to Superior late this afternoon."

"When will you come again? Can you stay overnight with us?" they both asked at once, all ready to make plans. "Next weekend? We'll cook hot chocolate and sit up all night and talk."

Maggie's shoulders slumped and her eyes got misty.

"I don't know," she said. "Probably not for another month." Mrs. Ecklund didn't like to let her go—every weekend she had a big cleaning project for her. She wasn't sure it would be even that soon.

Concern etched Mary's face. "It's such a long time till school gets out and you'll come home for summer vacation," she said. "I hope we don't have to wait that long to see you."

Summer vacation. Maggie stared blankly at her friends. Would she come back for the summer? She'd assumed she'd stay on as housemaid for the Ecklunds.

But there, summer would mean cleaning that big stone house from attic to cellar, with probably no time to go to the lake with Nancy and Suzy. She wasn't sure Nancy and Suzy would ask her along anyway—they weren't quite such good friends anymore. They'd grown apart, grown in different directions.

"Everyone come get a bag or a box," called Pastor Knudsen. "Christmas presents sent by the good folks in Rush City." So many folks, from so many places, had sent money and clothes and everyday household items to the survivors of the fire disaster, it warmed and healed Hinckley's hearts. Even more heartwarming was the pile of brightly wrapped presents and the good wishes that surrounded them.

Jack was first in line. The girls laughed, getting in line themselves. Maggie pushed difficult plans for her future to the back of her mind. Today was Christmas.

Back home again, Gramma unstuffed the goose, stirred gravy, and mashed potatoes while Maggie set the table, a lovely round oak table with several leaves, now covered with a mended linen cloth. The china plates were chipped and mismatched. Gramma explained people had donated things to the fire survivors from their own linen chests and china closets. She treasured every piece as if it were a family heirloom. Jack's big handsome calico cat watched approvingly from the top of the cupboard with her big green eyes, patiently waiting for cream.

The goose was a wild Canadian that Eddie had shot during late fall migration, and as there was already snow on the ground, it had been kept frozen on the back porch—under the rafters, out of Nero's reach—until Christmas. Jack had traded flour for wild rice from the Indian camp, and Gramma had gotten cranberries from the Anderson farm. She wouldn't tell where she had gotten the mincemeat.

* * * *

"Maggie, are you going to eat your pie?" asked Jack, fork poised. "You didn't finish your goose. Too full for desert?"

"Don't daydream the day away, Maggie," teased Eddie. "Presents are waiting."

Jack dropped his fork, pushed his chair back and headed for the parlor.

"Just a minute, young man," called Gramma. "When we've finished dinner and cleared the table, then we can open gifts."

One look at Jack's face made everyone hurry. Grabbing dishes, a serving bowl or two, they stacked everything in a tottering pile in the dry sink and gathered around the tree, a little Norway pine Eddie had brought from Pine City. On Christmas Eve, they had strung popcorn and cranberries into garlands to drape over the branches. Gramma had baked gingerbread cookies and Papa had brought apples and black walnuts, all hung on the tree with red yarn. The cat crept under the tree, batting playfully at a walnut that dangled within reach.

Gramma hadn't allowed candles, but there were a few ornaments donated by the Relief Agency. Maggie noticed a blown-glass ornament, a Father Christmas, that was almost like Mama's old one. Maggie wondered who would have donated such a precious ornament. Had it belonged to someone's family? To someone's mama?

Gramma clapped her hands, trying to quiet the boys. Gift opening was never as organized as Gramma wished. Paper tore, and ribbons ripped, and kisses and thank yous flew around the room.

Gramma had knitted caps and scarves and mittens, and Eddie had made skis and snowshoes, and Papa had brought home oranges and raisins and apples, and Jack had whittled and carved, and Maggie had sewed and embroidered and tatted. She'd had lots of long winter evenings in her room to make presents.

When there wasn't another unopened present to be found, Gramma brought out sugar cookies and apple cider, and Jack stomped around in his new baseball knickers and snowshoes, and Papa put on his new vest from Maggie and lit his pipe, and Eddie played carols on his new mouth organ. Maggie hugged the pillowcases Gramma had embroidered that matched her tattered sofa pillow from Mama. Bluebells and forget-me-nots. She sighed happily, inhaling the aroma of pine, cinnamon, and pipe tobacco.

And then Papa drew his railroad watch from his vest pocket.

"We'll have to leave for the depot soon, Missy," he said.

Jack stopped in midstomp. "Do you have to go?"

"Glad you came, little sister," Eddie said, his voice falsely cheerful.

Gramma's eyes grew sad. Her glasses seemed to slide down her nose. She shook out her new lace hanky.

Maggie stared at the clock on the shelf. It couldn't be time yet—but it was nearly three. She didn't want to go back to that lonely house in Superior! Cold and empty and lonely. She had hated leaving Superior to move to Hinckley, but leaving here was worse.

Being alone was worse.

Suddenly the locked doors in the back of her mind burst open. She didn't want to go back to Superior. Despite all her desperate clinging to her old home, her insistence that leaving Superior meant leaving Mama, she now knew that Mama lived in her heart, went with her wherever she went. She realized that she had felt Mama's presence here in Hinckley more than she ever had in Superior, especially during the scary times, the bad times. And she felt Mama here now, at Christmas, at the good times too. She needed to be here. Here was home. Gramma was right. Home is where the heart is.

Kneeling beside Papa's chair, she grasped his arm. "Papa, I don't want to go back. I don't want to live in Superior." She choked down a sob. "Being alone is so hard. Harder than I had thought living in Hinckley would be."

She had thought all the ghosts and nightmares and unwanted memories would haunt her here. Her eyes widened and a tear spilled over. Impatiently, she wiped her cheek. It was in Superior—only in Superior—where all that tormented her!

"Don't send me back, Papa," she whispered, her voice loud in the small quiet parlor. "I need to be here."

Seconds ticked off the clock. No one breathed.

Papa's hand stroked her hair. "It shouldn't be hard to arrange," he said, his voice husky. "I'll stop off at the Ecklunds and explain things."

Eddie cheered. Jack whooped and stomped. Laughter and tears and hugs erupted. Maggie's knees felt weak, and her tears flowed unchecked. It took quite a while before everyone settled back to cookies and cider. Papa left on his afternoon run but would return that night.

Quiet, comforting evening enveloped the parlor. Lantern light flickered, the stove crackled cheerfully, and a gentle wind outside sang a soft Christmas lullaby. Maggie curled into Papa's wing chair with the present he had given her, the book *Heidi*. The cat curled up on her lap, her paws kneading. Flipping through the pages of her book, Maggie's mind wandered.

Their lives had changed drastically since last Christmas back in Superior. She had been so unhappy moving to Hinckley. She'd made no effort to make it her home—had never missed an opportunity to let her family know how much she hated living here. And then she had nearly lost them.

Maggie straightened up in her chair, squaring her shoulders and disturbing the cat. It would all be different from now on. She would go to school with Mary and Clara and giggle and talk and stay overnight. She would go to Jack's baseball games and cheer and yell and flirt with the boys. She would go to dances with Eddie and meet his new friends.

And she would plant grass and trees and flowers and shrubs and make their home the prettiest in Hinckley.

REQUIEM
September 1, 1895

Barely a ribbon of light traced the horizon, and faint stir-rings from the chicken coop broke the dawn silence. Maggie closed the front door quietly behind her and sat on the porch step to put on her shoes. A warm nose nuzzled her cheek and a slobbery wet tongue licked her face.

"Nero," she whispered, "sit quiet." He obliged, leaning his bulk against her shoulder. Fastening the last shoe button, she put her arm around the big shepherd dog and scratched his ears.

The first rays of sunlight crept across the grassy lawn, setting the dew a-sparkle, the white picket fence the boys had built casting zigzaggy shadows. Maggie walked around the side of the house to check her flowers. She had planted so many seeds and shrubs and tree seedlings that Jack complained constantly about pumping water for her yard and for Gramma's garden. Maggie knew Jack complained mostly out of habit—rainfall had been normal this summer.

She closed the back gate behind her. "Better stay here, Nero," she said. "Jack will be looking for you." Trotting to the back porch, Nero stretched out across the doorway.

New boardwalks lined the streets of town. And to Maggie's delight, all the new buildings had been painted. The state legislature had provided free seeds, and every house had a grassy yard, planted with little trees, flowers, and gardens. Maggie walked past their new Swedish Lutheran church, just recently erected and "all paid for," as Papa boasted. On the opposite corner was the new Presbyterian church. Gramma was looking forward to the box social at the Catholic church.

Across the street, the new brick school proudly presided over an entire city block, surrounded by newly planted elm trees. It was built on the same foundation as the old one, using the same plans. Workmen had put in long hours to have it finished for the first day of school this year. Classes began next week. Maggie and Mary and Clara had already planned to walk to school together the first morning. And to join the chorus.

Walking on into town, Maggie passed the Town Hall. The fire station on the first floor housed the new Waterous Fire Engine. Today's memorial service would be held on the second floor. There would be no escaping memories today. Everyone would be together.

Everyone would remember and relive that day and the days after. Would that open old wounds, revive nightmares? Or would it help to share the pain and move on?

She sat on a bench in the adjacent City Park, which now had grass and picnic tables and small tree seedlings. Maggie hoped the trees would soon grow big enough for birds to nest in them. As if on cue, pigeons on the school roof cooed, and somewhere a meadowlark warbled.

Remembering Mama was not so hard anymore. The family talked of her often now, and it made them feel closer to her and to each other. When they shared their memories, the pain eased. Maybe the memorial service would do that for the town. Or maybe it would bring too much grief, too much suffering. Maybe some folks weren't ready to face those old wounds too openly. She bit her lip, wondering how she would react when brought face-to-face with remembered tragedy.

She took a deep, deep breath. Better to acknowledge the grief. Burying grief didn't get rid of it. Sharing it, embracing the comfort folks offered, healed it. If she'd learned anything at all, she'd learned that. A gentle smile returned to her face, and she stood, brushed her skirts smooth, straightened her shoulders, and walked home. Her real home.

Nero met her at the gate. The smell of fresh coffee and sizzling bacon wafted out the window and the sound of laughter beckoned her in. Papa and Eddie sat at the table, engaged in a lively discussion about Angus Hay's latest editorial. It seemed Angus had bragged about Hinckley's great farming opportunities on wide expanses of land that "nature had cleared."

Land sales were booming.

"Angus tends to get over-enthusiastic," said Eddie, "but he's right. Farming is great here. The crops—corn, oats, berries, vegetables—all thrive in the cleared ground. The yields are outstanding."

"Well, farming will replace lumbering here," said Papa. "Maybe that's a good thing. We need trade and industry to keep the railroads going through Hinckley."

Smiling at them, Maggie went out to the backyard and picked flowers to take to the cemetery.

* * * *

Gramma led the family to a row of wooden folding chairs near the front of the hall, Jack running in behind them just in time for a seat. A steady stream of visitors quickly filled the room. Maggie looked up at the raised platform, at the podium flanked with big bouquets of flowers. She gripped her handkerchief tightly. So did Gramma.

The building grew warm, and Gramma opened her fan. Subdued conversation buzzed through the crowd. The hall overflowed, latecomers standing outside.

Dignitaries walked in and found their places on the stage. Dr. Stephan smiled down at Maggie and Gramma.

The church choir stood and sang "Amazing Grace" in clear, poignant voices. The speaker's comments flowed over Maggie, a few statistics catching her attention: four hundred eighteen officially recorded deaths, although it was believed more than six hundred people had died in the firestorm.

"I don't think that includes Wacouta's village," whispered Jack. "Searchers found twenty-three bodies scattered along the path in the woods, but they left them there for their own people to find. Their families would want to bury them in their village, have their own ceremonies."

"In four hours, the holocaust destroyed four hundred square miles," the speaker intoned. With a jolt, Maggie's mind flashed back to the magnificent pine forests she had ridden through, to the wild animals and birds, the pristine lakes and rivers. People and houses weren't the only victims.

The choir sang again, "Faith of Our Fathers," their voices stronger, filled with conviction. A solemn hush settled as the clergy spoke.

"Disaster is a part of life on earth," they reminded the faithful. "But another life follows, where there is no more pain, no more sorrow, no more tears. And there our loved ones wait for us."

Muffled sobs punctuated the sermons, but a palpable feeling of peace and faith filled the auditorium. Maggie didn't need her handkerchief. Immediately following the ceremony, everyone walked to the cemetery. Jack ran ahead.

"There's Tony," he called back.

A neat wrought-iron fence enclosed the cemetery. Trees and hedges had been planted. Wild grapevines twined the wrought iron. Their leaves were already tinged with fall colors, their clusters of small dark purple grapes promising fall. Walking through the gate, Maggie reached over to touch a young lilac bush she had planted. In memory of Mama. All the family had helped plant it, and they watered it every Sunday after attending church.

The four long trenches had been mounded, sodded, and were covered with flowers. Everyone brought fresh-picked bouquets to lay on the graves, and the air was scented by tiger lilies and asters and phlox. A hum of bumblebees accompanied hushed voices. Maggie stepped up to the mound and placed an armful of fragrant yellow daylilies tied in a bundle with a green ribbon on the grassy slope, then stepped back beside her family. The choir sang again, many of the assembled people joining in.

"We will gather by the river . . . "

A speaker's voice quoted Angus Hay's editorial in the *Hinckley Enterprise:* "When we again hear the song of the birds in the summer, and the golden grain is being gathered in the autumn from the fertile soil around Hinckley, the tale of the Great Fire will still be told."

Sweet and tender notes of a dulcimer and a violin flowed over the people. Someone began singing, "What a Friend We Have in Jesus."

Maggie sang too, her lovely young voice carrying clear and strong through the brisk autumn air and on over the rolling meadows.

This had been a good day.

AUTHOR'S NOTE

The summer of 1894 in Pine County, Minnesota, was marked by months of drought and extreme heat. This, however, did not slow down the lumber industry, which slashed its way through the native pine forests of northern Minnesota and Wisconsin, leaving scattered behind them limbs, branches, treetops, and stumps, dry and dead on the forest floor. Forest fires were common, many of them thought to have been started by sparks from railroad engine smokestacks or by farmers clearing land by burning stumps.

The Hinckley fire was greatly intensified because of a temperature inversion, a layer of cold air over a layer of hot dry air. One or more small fires heated a column of air that broke through to the cold layer, causing a sudden furious firestorm. Many survivors reported seeing tornadoes of fire, flying fireballs, and burning objects, all components of a firestorm. They called it the "Red Demon." To many, it seemed like the end of the world.

The firestorm raced across Pine County, ravaging not only the town of Hinckley, but also Sandstone, Brook Park, Mission Creek, Miller, Partridge, and Finlayson. There were four hundred eighteen recorded deaths and an uncounted number of missing persons.

Four hundred eighty square miles of forest burned in Pine County, plus large areas in adjoining counties. All this occurred in four hours. The fire burned itself out in marshy areas near the Wisconsin border.

The three main avenues of escape are recounted in this book. About four hundred and seventy-five persons were saved on the combined Eastern Minnesota train driven by Engineers Best and Barry. The Limited passenger train of the St. Paul-Duluth Railroad, engineered by Jim Root, delivered about three hundred people to safety at Skunk Lake. Another estimated one hundred people took refuge in the flooded gravel pit in Hinckley. There were many heroes whose brave efforts resulted in the saving of many lives in so terrible a catastrophe.

Throughout the surrounding countryside, many others were saved by taking refuge in creeks, wells, and sometimes in open fields. Many others died in similar surroundings.

Maggie and her family are fictional characters. Their personalities, words, and actions are crafted to portray historical events. All other characters were real people. Their actions recount historical accounts. Some of their conversation is fictionalized, though much of it is taken from the survivors' personal accounts.

There is a Fire Museum in Hinckley, Minnesota, housed in the restored depot, which has an outstanding display of artifacts. One may also visit the gravel pit, Skunk Lake, and the cemetery, where the grass grows green and lush over four long mounds.

CITATIONS

The Hinckley Fire, by Antone Anderson and Clara McDermott, is a compilation of oral histories gathered from survivors. Tony's and Will's accounts of their survival are taken from their own words.

The editorial quoted from *The Hinckley Enterprise*, written by Angus Hay, was reprinted in *From The Ashes*, by Grace Stageberg Swenson.

BIBLIOGRAPHY

Akermark, Gudmund Emanuel. *Eld-Cyklonen*. Minneapolis: Companion Publishing Co., 1894.

Akermark, Gudmund Emanuel. *The Great Hinckley Fire or Eld-Cyklonen*. Translated by William Johnson. Askov, MN: American Publishing Co., 1976.

Anderson, Antone A., and Clara McDermott. *The Hinckley Fire*. New York: Comet Press Books, 1954.

Bylander, C. B. "Cyclone of Fire." *The Minnesota Volunteer*, July-August, 1994.

Larsen, Lawrence H. *Wall of Flames*. Fargo, ND: The North Dakota Institute for Regional Studies, 1984.

Leaf, Sue. "A Tale of Hubris from Early State History." *Minneapolis Star Tribune*, 28 August 1994.

Meier, Peg. "Amid Death, Wind, and Fire: Heroism." *Minneapolis Star Tribune*, 28 August 1994.

Nobisso, Josephine, and Ted Rose. *John Blair and the Great Hinckley Fire*. Boston: Houghton Mifflin, 2000.

Peterson, Clark C. *The Great Hinckley Fire*. Smithtown, NY: Exposition Press, 1980.

Swenson, Grace Stageberg. *From the Ashes*. St. Cloud, MN: North Star Press of St. Cloud, 1994.

A NOTE OF THANKS

I would like to thank my editor, Katy Holmgren, for her professional expertise and encouragement; James Cross Giblin and Pat Ramsey Beckman for mentorship and critique advice at the Highlights Foundation Workshop at Chautauqua, New York; and to Jane Resh Thomas, for guidance in the beginning of this novel in finding Maggie's inner voice and in finding the doorways to inner memories. Thanks also to the Hinckley Fire Museum, an excellent resource for research, and to the town of Hinckley for its preservation of artifacts, memories, and spirit.

Thanks also to the Arts Center of Saint Peter, Minnesota, for enthusiastic support, and the McKnight Foundation (through Prairie Lakes Regional Arts Council) for financial support, and to my family for their encouragement. And of course, my fond appreciation to the Night Writers of St. Peter.

And most especially, heartfelt thanks to Mary Casanova, Mentor Extraordinaire.

ABOUT THE AUTHOR

Jan Neubert Schultz lives with her husband on a farm homesteaded by the Schultz family in 1869, along the bluffs of the Minnesota River Valley. A fifth-generation Minnesotan, Ms. Schultz has been fascinated since childhood by the stories that have been handed down in her family and by the people and events that have shaped Minnesota's history.